A CLOSE FAMILY

By the same author:

Novels:

The Catalyst	1960	Faber & Faber
Personal File	1962	Faber & Faber
Now	1965	Faber & Faber

Story Sequence:

The Conjuring Show	1981	Alun Books

Science:

Glass	1956	Methuen
2nd edition, revised	1971	Chapman & Hall
Atoms and the Universe		
(in collaboration)	1956	Eyre & Spottiswode
2nd edition, revised	1962	Eyre & Spottiswode
3rd edition, revised	1973	Penguin

A
CLOSE
FAMILY

by

G O Jones

NEW MILLENNIUM

292 Kennington Road, London SE11 4LD

Copyright © 1998 G.O.Jones

All rights reserved. No part of this publication may be
reproduced in any form, except for the purposes
of review, without prior written permission
from the copyright owner.

British Library Cataloguing in Publication Data.
A catalogue record for this book is available
from the British Library.

Printed by Arm Crown Ltd. Uxbridge Rd, Middx.
Issued by New Millennium*
ISBN 1 85845 221 X
*An imprint of The Professional Authors' & Publishers' Association

1

I

Martin wondered whether he had drunk too much: he did not think he had. Quietly, without drawing attention to the fact, he left the party and went into the garden. It was dark, cool, and raining slightly. He tried to breathe deeply.

But he now felt ill in a new way: a pain in his chest shocked him. He decided to lie on the lawn: slowly, and carefully, he placed himself down. The moist grass against his cheek comforted him. He would wait there until he felt better, as he assumed he must, quite soon.

Later, he felt again the moist grass against his cheek and knew that he had fainted: he had not felt it happen. He was curiously happy. He felt, more clearly than ever before, the absolute need to live for ever. The pain had gone, but he was cold. He continued to lie for some minutes and then, testing himself, rose slowly and walked carefully into the house, brushing drops of water off his clothes. He had no spare flesh, but he now moved as though he had.

The party had changed its pattern. Some of the guests had gone: most of those remaining were in close groups, sitting on the floor and on chairs. The conversations had been taken over by leaders. He picked up a bottle of wine and moved toward one of the groups. One of his neighbours was speaking.

"Oh, no, I have no opinion. I just tell the underwriter what the assessors say. Then I tell the agent what the underwriter says. I'm the broker, you see. Of course, if I don't agree I sometimes suggest he asks for another opinion ..."

Martin moved to another group, filling glasses as he went.

"He's the kind of bloke who, if he gets his ass kicked, has to pass it on."

"It wasn't an ass-kicking session at all. He was just rather neurotic about it."

"He's insane, actually. But in a positive way."

Martin moved again.

"Well, there I am. I've got a superintendent, a manager, a general manager, a managing director, a chairman, and the owner. The question is: who's the boss?"

"He's somewhere along the line. I bet he knows it. I bet they all know it."

A guest had approached Martin and seemed anxious to talk to him. He looked tired, and was drunk, rocking a little. But he spoke clearly and slowly. Martin could not remember his name.

"Hello, Martin," he said. "Nice party."

"Glad you could come. We enjoy it too, you know," said Martin.

"You all right, Martin? Look a bit pale."

There was a pause. Martin had often had to talk to people whose names - and even identities - he had forgotten. One had to be cautious: questions must be generalised, not specific. One must avoid any form of words which demanded the use of a name. It was hard to do it elegantly.

"No, I'm all right, I think. Overdoing it, perhaps." He indicated the bottle in his hand. "What about you? How is it all going?"

"It's *boring*, Martin."

The guest rocked again; he had reached the point in his drunkenness at which he need not try to hide it. His talk came in spurts.

"Boring! That's what it is. Of course ... mustn't show it in court. 'Poor old Reginald', they'd say. 'On the slide'."

Martin remembered: his guest was a barrister.

"Shall I show you how it's done, Martin?" He put down his glass.

"Just watch." A sneer came over his face. He put both hands on a table.

"Do you *seriously* want the Court to believe that you knew nothing about it?" He waited, as though to give time for an answer, then appeared to stagger in disbelief.

"Are you quite sure that you understand what you are telling the Court?"

He waited again, then went on, as though tired.

"May I remind you that you're on oath? And so on ... and so on. Grown men!"

He sat, passing his hand over his face, as though in despair.

"Show the jury they're not to believe him. Then of course, up gets my learned friend. Now jig up and down. Make sure they see you ... whenever he says something you don't like. Show them they're not to take any notice."

"But Reginald, doesn't that sort of thing annoy the judge?"

"Does you good. Anyway, who's he? Just your jumped-up colleague. You don't imagine, Martin," he seemed to adopt his professional sneer, "that *that's* decided on merit?"

Martin wanted to encourage his guest.

"Reginald, I haven't seen your wife yet. How is she?"

The guest's expression hardened. He seemed to be one made fierce, not genial, by drink.

"Didn't you know, old boy?"

He rocked again.

"I thought everyone knew. I don't know how she is. I don't bloody care how she is ..."

"I'm sorry, Reginald. I didn't know anything."

Martin waited for a moment, signifying his sympathy, then moved away, excusing himself. As host, carrying wine, he was entitled to circulate among his guests. He must remember: if you haven't seen someone for some time, don't ask about his wife.

Across the room he saw his wife, Madge, with a new colleague of his, Tony Booth, and his wife. He and Booth had, so far, an uneasy relationship. He joined them; Booth's wife was speaking.

"Tony's an absolute softie," she said. "When we were coming here, looking for the house, an Arab stopped us. Not one of the wealthy ones. Just a poor Arab, or something like that. He was holding a piece of paper, and muttering something ... "

Booth looked embarrassed. "Cumduntum, Cumduntum ... " he said.

"That's right. 'Camden Town'! He just kept on saying it. So Tony looked at the piece of paper - it was a sort of map - and started to tell him how to get there. He seemed to be looking for a hostel. Quite hopeless, of course. Didn't understand a word. Just kept saying 'Cumduntum, Cumduntum'. So what does Tony do? Puts him in the car, and we drive back to Camden Town. Took ages to find it."

Martin had assumed that Booth and his wife were in a familiar mould: thrusting, careerist husbands often seemed to have charming, soothing wives. It was a deadly combination. He now wondered whether he might find, eventually, that he actually liked Booth. He hoped not: it would weaken his position. If Booth were to prove to be likeable, as well as younger, up-and-coming, perhaps a high flyer, he would be impossible to contain.

Madge linked her arm with his. "Let's go and talk to Jim and Alice," she said. They were friends; they had arrived late, as though - Madge had thought - uncertain whether to come. She had sensed a tension between them.

"How's the crack, Jim?" said Martin, and regretted it at once. It was some moments before Jim answered.

"As a physical entity, Martin, it's getting bigger. As a legal entity, we seem to be getting it under control."

He did not seem to want to talk about it, but having begun, he must continue.

"What our chap says is that both the original builder and our surveyor must be liable. The surveyor is trying to pin it on the builder, naturally. But apparently builders keep disappearing, or going bankrupt."

"But surely the only person responsible to you is your surveyor," said Martin.

"Yes, Martin," said Alice. "He's saying we didn't have a full survey."

Martin wished he could change the subject of their conversation. But Alice went on.

"Whatever happens ... whether we get the money or not ... the house has to be taken apart, practically."

"They just have to start again from the bottom," said Jim. "Someone made a 'mistake'." He used the inadequate word ironically. All became silent.

"How's everything else?" said Martin. Again, seeing his friends' faces, he regretted his question. Apparently puzzled, they seemed to say: what else was there?

Nearby another group were talking. Martin noticed their animation.

"It's the least rewarding of all arts," said one. "There they are, sometimes hundreds of them ... years of training, enormous dedication ... and desperate energy going into it, and you feel - nothing!" The subject was ballet.

Another in the group seemed to disagree. "Surely," he said, "that only shows that you, personally, are - so to speak - 'tone deaf' to it. If you did happen to respond to the movements themselves it would have a meaning for you ..."

Martin remembered something from many years before. Determined that his children be exposed to every art, he had taken them to concerts and plays. One afternoon he had taken his daughter Joan to a programme of Indian dance. The curious music, and the movements, conveyed nothing to him, but Joan had attached her little girl's concentration upon it all: that had delighted him.

About six dancers had come on the stage in a circle. Moving their heads, arms and hands, they flowed around the stage for minutes. One of the girls was a little slighter, perhaps a little younger than the others. He fixed his eyes on her, and was instantly captured, amazed at the beauty of her movements. He would have watched for ever. It gave a meaning to the rest. She flowed around, alone, a coloured figure in a black-and-white world.

It's magic, he had thought. It's the spirit of delight! I'm surprised by joy!

"We missed you for a time," said Madge, when the guests had gone. She and Joan were washing up, and talking about the party: it had gone well, on the whole.

"I wasn't feeling too good, as a matter of fact," said Martin. "I went out into the garden." He did not tell them that he had fainted, or about the pain.

They looked anxious.

"I'm all right now. Too much to drink, I expect."

They were not satisfied.

"Really, don't worry about it. Tired, I expect, and too much to drink ... and mixed them a bit, perhaps."

"Are you overdoing it, Dad?" said Joan.

"He is, actually," said Madge.

Again they looked anxiously, and severely, at him.

"Look after yourself, Dad," said Joan. Her expression denoted severity. But her eyes revealed anxiety.

"Don't bother with all this," said Madge. "We can manage it. Why don't you go to bed? I'll bring you a hot drink."

"Yes, Dad, go on. Go to bed."

He went upstairs. Undressing, he found his clothes sodden with sweat.

When Madge brought his drink she sat on the edge of the bed. She's really very contained, he thought. No spreading, no sagging; just a little grey at the edges. I suppose she'll start using rinses soon.

"Did *you* invite Reginald?" he said.

"No, Martin. I thought you must have."

"How odd! We hardly know him."

Both were puzzled. "He seems to be in a bad way," Martin went on. "His wife must have left him. And he badly wants to be a judge."

"Still, no harm done. Everything went off all right."

"Yes, but aren't parties funny! Isn't it odd to invite people to come to your house, all about the same time, all dressed up, and not for a *performance*, but just to stand up with drinks in their hands, then to find somewhere to sit with food, and all the time talking ... to each other! The mix is odd, too: neighbours, colleagues, or friends. 'One or more to qualify'. And gate-crashers, it seems."

"I must say," she said, "I didn't seem to have any new conversations - except with Tony Booth and Elizabeth. Whatever we talk about seems to be continued from last time."

"Yes," he said, "'Did you have any trouble getting here' ... *au pair* girls ... motor cars ... houses, dry rot, woodworm ... and of course children, children ... and they talk about our extraordinary house, and how good it is for parties."

It was a large house - the largest part of a much larger one split into several dwellings. It was because theirs included the original hall and staircase, and the sitting room, that it was good for parties. But it was an anxiety. Five families hoped that the great building, solidly made of excellent materials, but a hundred years old, would survive their ownership without disaster. Martin and Madge shared chimneys, party walls and gutters with all the others, and knew exactly their state. Every few years a chimney, or a gutter, would need to be replaced; some arrangement would be made with the neighbour concerned. They were not sure whether, on the whole, they were gaining or losing ground. At first, short of money, they had suffered sleepless nights and worried days, calculating and recalculating.

But it had been an article of their faith: there must be a substantial home. It would be a symbol of their marriage and of their family; it would be, they hoped, the centre of gravity of their children's memories, and a source of strength for them too.

"Then at the right moment everyone says it's been a lovely party; they go off, pull everyone to pieces and begin to wonder whether it isn't time they had *their* party."

She looked closely into his face. "You don't look too bad," she said. "Tired, I can tell. As a matter of fact, when you're tired, and a bit under the weather, you do, just about, look your age."

"That's exactly what getting old is. First you look your age when you're tired and under the weather. Then you just begin to look your age."

She made a dismissive gesture. "But Joan's right. She's worried about you. Why don't you take things easily for a bit?"

"Yes, I know, Madge. I will. I'll see to it."

"Really do, Martin."

"Say goodnight to Edward for me. He seems very quiet. Perhaps he's asleep."

"I will, Martin."

"It's sad about Jim and Alice. That crack - or something - it's tearing them apart."

"I know. Why don't we meet them for a chat: in a pub."

"Good idea, Madge. Let's."

*

On Sunday Martin served drinks to his sons Robert and John before lunch. Of the four children, only Joan and Edward now lived in the family home. John, at university, used it as his base during vacations, but was often away; Robert had clearly moved out. But hundreds of Sunday lunches had fixed the habit in their minds: although it did not often happen, this was still the time when they were most likely to meet. Sometimes one or other of the grandmothers might be there; the two grandfathers had died some years before, neatly and concisely.

"Tell me about Tom and Deirdre, Dad," said Robert. They were neighbours.

"Well," said Martin, "you're only a week behind us. We seemed to be the last to know. She must have been pretending ... for weeks, that nothing had happened. Coming over to borrow sugar, and that sort of thing. Perhaps she really came over to see if we knew. Then Tom rang me one night. He started off asking how I was, and how Mother was, but not going on to say anything, almost as though he was expecting me to. Then he said he'd like to have a talk, and I could tell it wasn't about our chimney, but more serious. So I said: 'why don't you come over'. He'd only have to get out of his front door, and into ours. And he said: 'but don't you know? I'm not *there*!' He started to laugh. Then he said 'didn't you know? I've taken up with Marjorie. Just like Mr Polly!'"

"Who said that, you or Tom?" said Robert.

"He did. So I said, teasing him, I suppose, as he seemed to be so cheerful about it: 'but Marjorie isn't a plump woman'. That set him off again. Then he said: 'no, she's quite thin, actually'."

"Well, I'm blowed," said Robert. "I'd never have thought it of him."

"It seems he suddenly walked out about three weeks ago and just moved in with Marjorie. Deirdre didn't know there was anything between them. I haven't seen him yet. I'm meeting him in the pub. Of course Mother has seen Deirdre and told her that we know. So now she hears all about it - one side of it, anyhow. It's certainly the event of the year. Tom and Marjorie are still only just down the road."

"How funny that he should laugh about it," said Robert. "But of course, how absolutely right."

"He was laughing his head off," said Martin.

"The point is," said John, "they were part of our childhood, like this house, and all the neighbours. They've always been there. We can't quite believe it."

"Keep us informed, won't you, Dad," said Robert.

"Do you still use my room, Dad? Would you like me to clear my things out?"

"Yes, Robert. I sleep there if I want to read in bed, or work late and just drop into bed."

Martin wondered whether Robert, at twenty-three, had at last relinquished his claim to the room. None of the children liked arrangements to be changed, even if they had no part in them: the parents had understood that they would, for a time, want both independence and security, and therefore had a continuing claim on the family home. But they would, eventually, be weaned from it.

"No hurry to take your things. And use it when you like, of course."

"Of course, Dad. I'll clear it out, some time."

"Did you know John was going to Switzerland again?"

The parents liked to make sure that each of the children knew what the others were doing. It sometimes seemed they were not sufficiently interested in each other.

"Expenses paid, John?"

"Yes, Robert. Working. In other words, swotting. I'm miles behind. At least ten books I haven't opened yet."

Martin knew it had been for him to hear. He had learnt how to listen to the children anxiously, but not too anxiously. It seemed to be one of their main needs. Another - at least he had assumed so - was to have invited an obvious rejoinder, and to have it not made. 'Why have I been paying fees all this time' he might have said. He wondered whether he, and Madge, had been wrong all along. Perhaps they should, always, have made the obvious rejoinder. It would, at least, have provided one sort of security.

"How's Mary, Robert?" said Martin. "We haven't seen her for some time."

"She's fine. I'll bring her around."

"See, Robert, Father approves of Mary," said John.

"Of course I do. I've liked all your girlfriends. And John's, as a matter of fact."

"Of course you have, Dad. We've noticed the graded seals of approval. And what about you, John? Have you got a current, accredited girlfriend?"

"Of course he has," said Martin.

"She's a nice girl," he went on. "Why don't you bring her some time?"

"Which one do you mean, Dad?" The three laughed.

"She's Sandy, isn't she?"

"Yes, Sandy."

"Well, why not bring her?"

Martin could not get out of the habit, in talking to his children, of weighing his words. He did not know why he still did it. Their conversation was genial, half teasing and half serious. But he knew that everything he said had been through some kind of censorship before he said it. The children did not seem to have the same inhibition. Or did they? He was not sure.

"Really, Dad," said Robert, "you - and Mother - you're the archetypal liberals. Why didn't you call us Julian and Jonathan?"

He adopted an exaggerated, actor's manner.

"No, Julian, I'm not *telling* you to stop rubbing the bread and butter into the wallpaper. I'm only saying that it will put Professor and Mrs Thompson to a lot of inconvenience to have to clean it up, and perhaps they won't invite us again. That would make Mummy and me very sad ..."

Surely, thought Martin, it was a sign of maturity that Robert was able to tease him. He had always assumed that parents teased children.

"No, Jonathan," went on Robert, "this is not a play-room. This is a shop, where they sell things - for all little boys' play-rooms. See, this lady and gentleman want to show it to their little boy ..."

"What's wrong with Mr Hutton?" said Robert at lunch. He was another neighbour. "He seemed to be avoiding my eye when I came up the path."

"Well, yes," said Martin. "As a matter of fact, we did have a little ... argument."

"Go on, Dad!" said Joan. Again she looked severe, but not now anxious. "Why should you row with him? Surely he's quite harmless!"

It was not quite true. It was the chimney shared with Mr Hutton which gave most trouble.

"Quite ridiculous really. I was mowing the lawn, and turning every time I came to his fence. Some grass went over on to his flower bed - just a few blades. He must have been looking out of his window. He came out, carrying a little brown-paper bag, and started to pick them up, one by one, and put them in the bag. I said: 'Oh, Mr Hutton, I'm afraid some of my grass has gone over on your side'."

"And guess what he said," said Joan.

"'Do me a favour'," they chanted. "'Fair enough'."

Mr Hutton, a German by birth, had tried too hard to acquire, and use, the idiom of his adopted country. The children had noticed it quickly.

"No, not this time. He just looked up, looking very baleful, really, and said: 'quite frankly, Professor Blake, yes they have'."

All laughed. Joan abandoned her severity.

"But what did you say then, Dad?" said Joan.

"Never mind what I said." They laughed again. The children had always seemed to be fascinated by their neighbours, and by their parents' relationships with them. It almost seemed that they needed to observe how parents behaved with other people.

"You put it right for me, Joan. He thinks you're charming. As a matter of fact, he thinks you're all charming. It's just me he's doubtful about."

It was true. Years before the children had encountered the Huttons strangely. They had discovered that their own coal cellar ran underneath their neighbours' kitchen. They had begun to devise tricks which could be played from below: they would be innocent tricks - perhaps there would be smoke, or smells, or mysterious sounds. But before they could begin they had heard the sounds of a quarrel above them and stopped to listen. They had been amazed at the squalid, ungenerous accusations thrown from one to the other.

"That's all I am to you," Mrs Hutton shouted. "A *prostitute*." His answer could not be heard. But then his anger mounted and he began to shout too.

"You *tricked* me. You only wanted me to marry you." He began to speak more quietly and again could not be heard.

"You make me sick!" she shouted.

For a time it had been a sport for the children, but they had tired of it. They were a little ashamed of having listened, but also puzzled. It was known that the Huttons had been lucky to escape from Germany. But now they seemed to have set up their own concentration camp, to have wasted their good luck.

So the children had been sympathetic, and had connived at the world's deception. They could not understand why the Huttons stayed with each other, and how they could bear to walk in the park nearby, as they often did, arm-in-arm. It must be a part of the mystery of adult life, a curiosity of the married state.

"Did you know Father's getting a medal?" said Madge.

The children turned to him with cries of surprise.

"Really, Dad!"

"Just a medal, Robert. I've got to give a special lecture, and then get this medal."

"How often does it happen? Is there one every year?" said Joan.

"That's right. It's my turn this year."

"No question of 'turn'," said Madge.

All were pleased; they closed ranks around the theme. "I was wondering when something like this would happen," said Joan. "You seem to work very hard, Dad ... and you've been at it a long time."

Martin knew that he had the respect of his children. It was because, one by one, they had recognised that he was a sort of teacher. They had been conditioned to respect teachers. But it amused him that Joan had named the two things which did not count. However, he too had been pleased: he had known that in a few years' time it might have been too late.

"What about you, Mother?" said Robert. "Will you be getting a medal for Chinese Art?"

"Probably," said Madge.

"Well, what's next? Peloponnesian Wars ... Flower Arranging ...?"

"Take no notice of him," said Joan.

"Ah well," said Madge, "it's inevitable, I suppose, having failed to be properly educated, that I should try to fill some of the gaps. Perhaps I'll try a course in child-rearing."

"When are you going to ask me about my boyfriend, Robert?" said Joan.

"He's a nice boy," said Martin, "as a matter of fact."

"I mean," went on Joan, "that it's about time that Robert, as the family's senior tease, turned his attention to his little sister. And if he waits, he'll see a spotty youth calling for me about three o'clock."

"You don't mean Steve, surely!" said Madge. "That's not how I'd describe him at all."

"Oh, Mother!" said Joan. "You - and Dad - you really are such mother-and-father figures. Not actually spotty, Robert. But definitely a youth. Just a sixth-former, like me."

"I didn't say a word," said Robert. He turned to Edward.

"You're very quiet, Edward."

"As usual, Robert."

"Did you know," said Joan, "Granny doesn't go out at all now. She's afraid of being mugged. I tried to say that was silly, but of course she knows someone who has been."

She was Madge's mother and lived in London. "I won't say 'why don't we have her here'," went on Joan, "because I know it wouldn't be me who'd have to look after her."

Again Robert assumed his actor's voice.

"But Samantha, the fact is that Granny *is* getting rather old, and doesn't like living in a house with other people ..."

"That's not funny," said Joan.

"Isn't it just that she thinks everything's getting worse because she's old?" said Edward.

"It is getting worse for her, of course," said John.

"Of course old people think things are getting worse," said Martin. "Mother and I are trying to resist it. So we don't really know whether they are or not. As a matter of fact, we don't know what we think about most things now. I don't, anyhow."

It was true that Martin, chronologically middle-aged, sometimes found it hard to define, or even to discover, his attitudes to the controversies of the day. It was as though, age being clearly the main determinant, he could not decide at what age to stand. 'Muggers', who were usually young, often black, drew sympathy from the young because they were assumed to be disadvantaged; they drew a guarded sympathy from him too. But he could not bear to use the word: it seemed to him that to accept the word was to authenticate the fact.

The police, however, drew no sympathy from either side. "The only way," Martin had once said to Madge, "to find out where you really stand is to set up a trick question for yourself. Imagine there's to be an enquiry into whether police showed brutality on some occasion, and you know nothing about the facts. You know at once what you want the verdict to be, and you've made *that* decision without the facts". It had relieved him that he had passed that test: he would have wanted an adverse report.

"The trouble with you," said Robert, "is that you blind yourself."

"You too."

"That's Dad's way of saying," said Joan, "that we blind ourselves to different things."

"Very good, Joan," said Robert.

"*Are* things getting worse?" said Edward.

"Well no," said Robert. "Apart from the fact that we'll probably all be blown up, things are getting better."

"A typically insensitive remark," said Joan. She was angry because she had seen that Edward had wanted an answer.

"Not that insensitive," said John. "Possibly true, even."

"Anyway," said Edward, "*statistically*, the chance of being mugged is minute."

"It depends where you are," said John.

"When is Dad going to start taking it easy?" said Joan. She was severe again, not looking at him. The others turned to him.

"Yes," Martin said. "I'm going to. I'll take a day off sometimes." He took out his diary.

"Thursday. I'll take Thursday off. Perhaps I'll drive down to the Forest."

"What's so special about the Forest?" said Joan.

"Why don't you come with me, Madge?"

"I can't Thursday. Why don't you make it Friday? I could come then."

"I have to go in on Friday. Never mind. I'll just take things easily. Perhaps go to the Forest, perhaps stay around here."

"Ought you to go driving?" said Joan.

"Don't worry, Joan. Driving's no problem, as long as it's not too far."

"I'll make you sandwiches," said Madge.

"I'll be all right, Madge. I'll find a pub ... or something."

"You will be making sandwiches for John, won't you, Mum," said Joan. "To take to Switzerland, I mean."

Madge aimed a mock blow at her. "How will he manage?" went on Joan. She turned to John. "I hope you do manage, love."

Later, Martin and Madge talked about their children.

"They take exams," said Martin, "or have jobs; they have normal girlfriends, or boyfriends; they bring them here sometimes; they even seem reasonably concerned about us. And all around we see our friends' disasters. Drugs, dropouts, cults, *anorexia nervosa*, young daughters staying out all night ..."

"I put it down to you," said Madge. "Your steadiness. Of course they laugh at it, and pretend to despise it."

"No, Madge, it's you. You're always around, if they happen to want you - very serene, and solid if they happen to need that. And they've had remarkably little to rebel against, really."

"I think that's one thing they might have liked different."

Martin laughed

"When we're together, they push each other - and us, but not too hard. We do seem, as a matter of fact, to be in a quiet period." He pretended to touch wood.

"What were we hoping for? Just more of the same? Marriages, families, careers ..."

"Grandchildren, perhaps?"

The telephone rang. "Oh dear," said Madge. "That'll be Deirdre. I'll take it upstairs."

She was away a long time.

"What's the latest?" said Martin, when she came back.

"Well, first of all, she's now saying that Tom strangled her cat."

"Strangled her cat! What's the point of that? He's living with another woman. If she wants a divorce she'll get it. Anyway, it's not a marital offence to strangle your wife's cat, is it?"

"What she said was: 'I now realise it must have been Tom'. It's just to show what a heel he is. She also said Jim and Alice were splitting up."

"Surely not! Not Jim and Alice too!"

"I think she wants it to be true, so that ... hers doesn't seem so unusual."

"Of course, it does rather spread. It's a sort of chain reaction. Analogies seen by everyone. Subjects brought up that otherwise wouldn't be."

He paused.

"As a matter of fact, I wouldn't have expected it of Tom and Deirdre. Or rather, of Tom. He likes to be a pillar of society. I'd have thought he'd be the last to walk out."

He paused again.

"You just ... can't tell about anyone."

"Deirdre says he's absolutely *neurotic* about money. She goes on about it rather."

"They've both always struck me as rather obstinate."

"I don't think either of them puts much effort into their marriage," she said, a little severely.

"Well ... you just can't tell. From outside."

They were silent for a time. The theme was obviously one of interest to them, but did not seem to be one of danger. It could be dropped, or resumed.

"Did *we* row a lot?" she said. "I can't remember too well. At least, I can't remember what about."

"I do remember ... that we did have rows."

"What happened to them? Did we sort out - whatever it was - or did they just dissipate?"

"Just dissipated, I think. We were probably both hoping for signs that the other didn't want to go on, and they usually came."

Turning his mind back to the matter, he remembered more. At first he could not have believed, when they had been locked in one of their angry quarrels, that they could ever get out, could ever have kindly feelings for each other again. Later, these had become times of communication. How strange, he thought, that we don't seem to remember.

"Did I tell you," he said, "Tom wants to meet me at the pub. I said I would. I've an idea he wants to find out how things are ... going." He inclined his head in the direction of their neighbours' home.

"I see quite a lot of Deirdre," she said. "She finds any excuse to come over and talk. Like asking if I'll look after the kids some day *next* week so that she can go to her solicitor."

"I suppose we'll help any way we can. Talk to them both, of course, but not be the channel of communication: not tell one what can be quoted to the other."

"Let's see how it goes. Of course I said yes. I've told her I'll look after them any time. They won't go to anyone who doesn't know about Tom."

"I must say," she went on, "it riled me a bit to see him in the park, with his new girlfriend. He had his jacket over his shoulder: they looked like a couple of young lovers. And just a few hundred yards away there were those kids - afraid to go out! They look *stricken*: just like little birds."

"I suppose I'll get a bit more of the picture from him."

"Have you thought," said Madge, "that we might really begin to think of a smaller house? You know, next year there'll only be Edward, probably. We're starting to rattle a bit already."

"I do sometimes think that. The children would hate it, of course."

"I know. They'll always want us to be here, just in case they want to come and see us."

"I always used to think home was really for them, not for us. Now I'm not quite sure who it's for."

It was not, he thought, that the children might want to return to the family home, to live there for a time. But there had to be somewhere to which they did not return, which they had left. When Robert had been mutinous, it had seemed to Martin that he needed their home as a base for his mutiny, somewhere to have mutinied from.

"It's for them, Martin."

"We really must see Jim and Alice," said Madge later.

Martin nodded. The form of words could be used with different inflexions. In the way in which she had said it, both knew that they meant to do it.

II

Robert belonged to the alternative society which the young had themselves created, straying from accredited paths imaginatively - and far more radically - than their parents' generation had been able to do. He had dropped out of the educational system as soon as it had seemed to point him in a direction; he had left home and he had, more or less, supported himself since. Martin and Madge never knew exactly what he was engaged upon, but remembering their own parents, they would not doubt him. They were grateful that he seemed not to be alienated from them - only from what, presumably, they must represent.

They envied him the confidence which had allowed him his freedom of action. In one bound, it seemed, the young had thrown off their fetters; it was, surely, their sexual freedom that had allowed it. Martin and Madge knew that that had been where fetters had held them. Robert seemed always to have girlfriends: sometimes he would bring one home. They were attractive, contemporary girls, obviously as free as he was.

But it seemed that even among the privileged young he was privileged. Something in his appearance had marked him out: he had only to wait, and the most desirable girls around him would indicate that they were interested. When he made the slightest move they were his. He had seemed to make the most of it, but to take it lightly. It was a family joke; in the times it was a sign of superior adaptation. Parents, used to the older system, could assume that he would, eventually, settle down. Perhaps, more experienced than many, and apparently less anxious, he would make a stable marriage.

It was not how it seemed to him. He was deeply anxious. His physical beauty had made his life harder.

He worked in a community theatre; its aims encapsulated those of the alternative society, would have served to define them. He thought that he had, at last, found his ideal environment, and hoped he could stay in it for ever. It was full of girls; many of them he desired.

Sometimes, looking at a girl, he would be captured by something in her face. It was partly in the eyes, and partly in the mouth - in the minute configurations of her lips - or perhaps in a disaccord between the two. He was not sure what it all signified: was it innocence, pity, or hurt? Whatever it was, it melted him, and he desired the girl.

But too often, before he was ready, the girl projected her sexuality upon him; she might use her face - exaggerating what she must know to be there - or she might approach him more closely, or more quickly, than she would have done to another. At once he felt, quite consciously, the instinct to withdraw. Ashamed, he would recover and pursue the girl. Sometimes, knowing that he must be the pursuer, he pursued when he had not desired. So he had captured girls, one after another. Mary was one of these.

But he had lost them. They saw in his eyes that a part of him was absent, and for their own protection, they moved away. What was left was not enough. Perhaps, he thought, only vanity had been left, and perhaps it was only vanity which had impelled him to capture them. But he would not admit it: he still hoped that he could sort himself out. The familiar phrase was comforting. It was always too late. Now, when the girl had gone, he went through the tortures of lost love, despising himself. He was not sure how he stood with Mary. He envied John his obvious ease in the matter.

So he reassured himself with work, throwing himself into it. Since he did not claim a talent, but only energy, he knew that it was energy that he must use. He had begun to be known, to formulate a career for himself, to find a purpose in what he did. Success in his work could excuse other failures, could be thought to be their reason.

A new recruit in the theatre, Connie, had shown him, very quickly, that she favoured him. She had spoken in code; there were others near, but she had spoken quietly, had meant only him to hear. It was the first moment of crisis: he had learnt how to handle it, trained himself not to withdraw.

"Let's go for a drink when this is over," he said. They went on to his flat. Without waiting, she threw her arms around him and kissed him; he felt distaste at the open, wet mouth, resentment that she was performing her own rite, in which he was not involved.

She laid a towel on the floor and drew him down upon her. He noticed the thickness of her thighs and the smallness of her breasts. He felt nothing. But from some level, deeper than his inhibition, and his vanity, his body took instruction.

He hoped there would be no conversation. They got into bed. He thought, not about her, or his easy conquest, but about himself. He must get sorted out. He envied Connie her simplicity, her directness, her absolute and uncalculating involvement. She seemed curiously innocent as well as practised. He supposed that she was, for the time being, fulfilled and satisfied, perhaps supremely happy: he envied her all that.

He had scored one more. But now he was sorry for her. He must not show it - he thought he had not yet done so. He would finish the evening cheerfully, and tactfully. He did not know what would follow, but he hoped she would not stay the night. He doubted whether this was the girl with whom he would sort himself out. He felt no desire, no love. He had been trapped again by his vanity.

*

John, unlike Robert, had seemed to remain on an accredited path. He had been swept from school to university; his ostensible purpose was to become a mathematician. His true purpose, known only to himself, was to find, and succeed with - whatever that might mean - a wonderful girl. It had not yet happened: ordinary girls would not do.

He had remained in the system because that had been the easiest course: it had relieved him of the need to think of another, had allowed him time to elaborate his fantasies, and to try to turn them into reality.

His quest was not straightforward. Though outgoing in intention, he was shy and diffident in performance. But surely, he thought, the right - the perfect - girl would see through his diffidence. His courage would be enhanced: he would become, like nearly all the human race, the *owner* of ecstasy.

In the first years of his puberty he had assumed that it was idealism - his fastidiousness, his honesty, his insistence upon perfection, or at least excellence - that restrained him. Now he knew it was shyness, but he was not sure of its cause. Was he afraid of failure? Or was he afraid, simply, of the reality? The answer did not rise to his conscious mind. Sexual love was so overwhelming, in anticipation, that it surprised him that those of his friends who had experience of it had seemed unchanged. He wondered whether they had truly understood the depth - the real significance - of their experience.

His emotional life existed on two levels. On one, the level of fantasy, his mind was filled with anticipations, imaginations - but always about real, actual girls. One after another the wonderful girls, encountered at tennis courts, at parties, or in classes, took over his being. On the other, the level of reality, they destroyed him by casual remarks, or by indifference. It was a fortunate, less painful end, when the casual remark had clearly revealed unworthiness: too often it did not. Either way, he would be driven back to the ordinary girls whom he could handle. So his emotions shuttled between hope, in the pursuit of a particular girl, despair after his failure to win her, and self-contempt when he transferred his pursuit to someone he considered unworthy. Unexpectedly, the tennis club had become an arena: he had joined because of one wonderful girl, but had lost her. She still played there, but not with him.

He did not know whether it was the same for others: the boasting of his stag friends gave no clue. But he had observed unexpected pairings and wondered whether they, too, might reflect compromise - by one or other. He could not discuss it with anyone, least of all Robert, the successful one. Books of instruction warned that there were hazards everywhere, but did not seem to deal with those which faced him.

His absorption in the world of girls was the most important thing in his life; he grudged the hours when, studying, or otherwise fettered, he must pretend to deny its importance. And yet, it was a sort of curse.

Was it not the same for everyone? It did not seem so. Otherwise the civilised, efficient world could not have come into being. It must be that the obsession faded eventually - through satisfaction, or loss of hope.

But his idealism remained, even though he suspected its motive. He could still distinguish between the wonderful girls - possessing some combination of beauty, spirit, and intelligence which captured his imagination - and the others, who possessed only oppositeness of sex. He would continue his quest, for ever if he must, until he found and won his own, undisputed, wonderful girl.

He knew, instinctively, that the true experience must be a realisation, with that wonderful girl, of all his sexuality, mounted to its peak, and personalised in her. All the sexual feelings he had experienced - the burgeoning excitements with *au pair* girls carelessly left at home, with saucy girls in dark corners, his instantaneous recognitions of female beauty, his response to mysterious qualities of eye, or body, and his idealism - all must reach their culmination through her. With luck the same must happen for her, through him. He still hoped for it all, though he knew it was a tall order.

Not only did he grudge the hours he must spend in study, he could hardly bring himself to secure them. He hated the intrusion they made into his real life. Why could it all not be deferred until later, when time would be less precious? So his plan to spend the vacation in Switzerland was one of desperation - a last bid to placate, before it was too late, the world of examinations, careers, success. The fragility of his determination was only too evident to him. But, he thought, once in the chalet, there could be no possible distraction. He imagined the calm mountains as providing the occasion for the concentration which he needed. He saw himself at last coming into sympathy with his text-books, at last seeing some point, even some joy, in the discipline to which he had notionally, and irresponsibly, committed himself a few years before - the cruel destroyer of time, and the limbs of girls.

As he set out on the journey, by boat and train, he was glad of the few days' reprieve before he must start work. It did not occur to him that he might look at his books on the journey: his irrevocable decision was enough for the moment. He felt free, freed even from the pressures of his curse. They could be exorcised only by certainty, continuity, fulfilment: he was not looking for adventure. He had not the confidence, could not generate the speed, would be overtaken by some shallow youth. And even if he were to succeed, for him it must not be an adventure, but the start of certainty, continuity, fulfilment, and he had not the time.

But he could not help but notice how many beautiful - perhaps even wonderful - girls travelled with him on the boat. It almost seemed that it must be the most beautiful who travelled. They were young, many of them schoolgirls, and unpartnered - French, German, Scandinavian, even English - unconscious of their charm and beauty, and therefore the more charming and beautiful.

He was relieved to be sharing an alcove with a young couple who were obviously together. At first he was puzzled by the youth's demeanour: he seemed to hold his head quite still, looking forward and slightly downward. John realised at last why he did not move his head: he had no need to because he was blind. It seemed that he must be newly blind: he had none of the skills which, John assumed, every blind person must eventually learn, and he seemed to depend absolutely on the girl. She seemed calm, happy and undistressed. She was not one of the beautiful, but whole and confident, in the manner of her generation.

The two were talking, quietly. She turned suddenly to John. "He's a jealous tit," she said. But she still seemed calm and undistressed.

John did not speak.

"He doesn't like me to talk to any other boy," she went on, "and I have to tell him that he mustn't be like that. See, Harry?" She turned back to him.

"I'm Josie, this is Harry," she said, turning to John again. "We're having our thing about jealousy. Sorry to embarrass you."

"I'm John. I wasn't embarrassed. But I was taken aback."

"Why, John?" said Harry.

"Well ... it seems so marvellous ... that you are obviously together, and very close, otherwise you wouldn't be travelling ... and if you are really not getting on ... Of course, it's not my business ..."

"We are close," said Harry, "and she's marvellous. We both understand why I'm suspicious, but I don't want to pretend I'm not."

"And I don't want to change," she said. "There's no-one like Harry, and we get on fine. Just occasionally we have this ... workout."

"But surely ..." John began. He could not understand how the couple, admitted, as they must be, into the full reality of love, could allow it to be prejudiced. Did they not realise the value - the real significance - of what they possessed? And although he must not say it, it seemed to him, too, that the girl's willingness to remain with her blind partner must prove that she was superior, even exceptional - a prize not to be risked.

He stopped: questions could only reveal his naivety. But he liked the couple and wanted to talk to them.

"Where are you going?" he said.

"We're going to India," said Josie. "We're learning Hindi." She seemed unfrightened by the enormity of their journey, or by the expectation of what they would find when they arrived.

"India! Why?"

"Because it's different," said Harry. "*Really* different. We're not drug addicts, or cult followers. We don't even think that we'll find wisdom. We decided, because of this," he showed that he meant his blindness, "to go just about as far away as we could."

"For how long?"

"We don't know. Until we're ready to come back, I think."

"The thing is, John," he went on, "we seem to be *sharing* my ... blindness."

Josie put her arm through his. "He had an explosion," she said. "He's a chemist. At least he was."

"We both seem to like you, John," she went on. She reached out her other arm and grasped his hand.

"See, Harry, I'm holding his hand."

Harry said nothing at first, as though unwilling to be tested. "Thanks for telling me." His tone was humorously ironic, not bitter.

"Where are you going, John?" he said.

"I'm going to Switzerland. But it's not a holiday. I've exams coming up - mathematics - and I absolutely have to work. So I've booked a chalet. It's now or never, as a matter of fact."

"But why go abroad, John?"

"I just have to go somewhere, Harry. There are too many ... distractions at home. And I won't know anyone where I'm going. I'm easily distracted, as a matter of fact."

"We used to travel a lot. We'd have our guide books, and read up about the country. But then I began to realise we were really only going to see *buildings*. I began to be very angry about the phoniness of buildings."

"Phoniness!"

"The building bears no relation to what's inside, John. Of course, you could say - since most of them are old anyway - that they don't have to. Perhaps they did when they were built."

"It's one of his things," said Josie. "I still love the phony buildings - for their beauty, even for their permanence."

"She used to positively ... thirst to see some building again," said Harry. "Like the belfry at Bruges. 'Can't we go back that way?' she'd say. And we would, of course. But John, just think of buildings today, and what's actually in them: even if there isn't corruption there'll be indifference ..."

"Of course I agree with that," said Josie.

" ... and they might be marvellous, inspiring architecture."

"What else, John?" said Josie suddenly. "What about your girl?"

"Josie, if I had a ... real girl, I'd be trying to forget about her for the present. But I haven't. Of course, I know a lot of girls, but I haven't got a ... *girl*."

"I thought so." Josie still held his hand. For the time being, he knew, a small part of her warmth had been diverted toward himself. The touch of her hand was its symbol. He knew it was only a small part, and was astonished how it moved him. He tried to give no sign. But how marvellous, how incredible, to have such a girl for oneself - to have the whole of it!

"As a matter of fact, Josie, I think if I really had a girl I'd find it easier to put all that out of my mind. It's because I haven't that I'm so easily ... distracted."

"You shouldn't have too much trouble," she said. "Nice person, nice blond hair, gentle face. Good-looking, if not handsome."

"I wish you'd tell me how to set about it, Josie."

All laughed.

"Would you take me to the Gents, John?" said Harry. "That's one thing she can't do - at least not yet. I wouldn't put it past her."

"Of course." He relinquished Josie's hand, to lead Harry away.

Later, the couple tried to sleep. It was dark. The boat trudged along monotonously; one by one the beautiful girls turned into untidy bodies. But John could not sleep.

By their talk the two had confirmed what he had at first guessed: they had indeed been admitted into the full reality of love. They had been willing to share a little of it with him. They had warmed him by their seriousness, had admitted him instantly into friendship.

But the warmth Josie had bestowed on him was a different kind of thing altogether. He could not understand why he had been so moved by it. Her gesture had been made, in part, on behalf of herself and Harry, and as a sign of their unity. But she had made it because she was a girl. It was significant because she was a girl: he had received a small part of her sexuality. Here lay the secret answer to all his questions.

He knew he would not see them again, after the crossing; to have attempted to do so would have been false. He had liked Harry, but it was Josie he would have wanted to see, and she was quite committed. The occasional gesture would have racked him. How strange that she had been able to show, instantly, that she was one of the wonderful. How despicable it had been to waste time on Sandy, his tennis partner, and the others.

After he had left the couple he felt the pain of a broken love affair. He knew, from experience, that it would take him some time to get over it. It had lasted only minutes and had consisted, overtly, of her single gesture. He was impatient with himself. Surely he must be abnormal! Surely no-one else could be so vulnerable. Anyone would have thought that, at twenty, he had never before touched a girl's hand.

His determination hardened. He would devote his whole being to his work until the examination. But as soon as that was over he would set about meeting the other - the real need of his life: nothing must stop him finding, and winning, his own perfect girl. Perhaps he would come abroad again.

Sleeping and waking, fitfully, on his long train journey, his thoughts oscillated between these and the immediate, and physical memory of the touch of Josie's hand.

*

Joan went to a girls' school, famous for its entry to Oxford and Cambridge colleges, infamous among the liberal middle class for its rearguard action against the developing comprehensive system. It had turned into a fortress, its stand at first unnoticed but now only too obvious. Martin and Madge were glad that they did not have a second daughter, and would not be forced to a new decision.

But the school, either ignorant, or careless, of the opinions of its parents, was also ignorant, or careless, of the leading interest of its population. It did not know the strength of its other enemy: it could not have guessed that it was itself a forcing ground for sexual education, as a mixed school, with the ostensible objects of interest in full view, might not have been. The girls, ripe, eager, and intensely interested, absorbed the sophisticated sexual morality of the times from each other, equipping themselves - without too much distraction - for their encounters in the real, daily world outside. Their presumed allies were the young married women teachers, who must be at least experienced; their presumed enemies were the older women who had begun their careers when few women teachers married. One or two men teachers added a piquant interest.

Around Joan not only the world, but her closest friends, were deeply involved - in theory and sometimes in practice - in love and sex. At the age of puberty everyone in the class had known who had begun to menstruate and who had not. To have begun was to join the club: to be early, or late, was to be thought precocious, or abnormal.

Her close friend, Brenda, had at fifteen been so passionately in love with a boy, and so hurt by his disinterest, that she already thought she had given up love, would never have to bear that pain again. But she put it down to bad luck, and did not try to persuade Joan.

Walking home from school, they talked about their headmistress. She had, that afternoon, called together the whole of the Sixth Form: it was always ominous. Had girls been seen in the local cafés after school, and perhaps smoking? Or was the Sixth to be asked to show an example to their juniors in some other area - games, perhaps?

There were a number of such items. She had appealed to the girls to help her, to realise the importance of their rôle as seniors. As always, they listened courteously: it was a famous school. She had shown that she was nervous as she came to her last item.

"I did not expect, girls, to have to speak about ... one matter." The girls became quiet.

"I have been shocked to hear ... and I hope it is not true ... that some of you ... I was told as many as a half, though I simply cannot believe it ... have *lost their flower!*"

Repeating the phrase, Joan and Brenda could not contain themselves.

"Flower!" said Brenda.

The girls had remained quiet; the headmistress had gone on, but she had not invited comments.

"What does she know about it?" said Joan.

"How did we keep quiet?" said Brenda.

"Nothing about *relationships*."

"Anyway, who told her?"

"It'll be some parent." Both agreed.

It was reasonably obvious. A girl would have made the accusation in her own defence. Her shocked parents would have told the headmistress. The natural lines of defence had been breached.

"Let's hope she drops it, Brenda. We don't want letters to all the parents. It's the sort of thing she might do."

"But surely, Joan, yours are all right?"

Joan thought for a moment.

"But Brenda, they don't know about Bryan, and I don't want them to."

"No, I know you don't."

"I don't exactly know why. If I told Father, he'd probably

swallow and say that I knew best. He'd really think it wasn't his business. Then he'd go away and worry."

"Would he tell your mother?"

"Of course not! I'm not sure what would happen if I told her."

"Of course," she went on, "I'd hate it if they just found out. They wouldn't understand."

"Wouldn't they, Joan?"

"How could they? They must have forgotten what it's like."

Joan and Brenda lived near each other. It comforted both mothers to know that they were close friends. If one did not arrive home after school, she would be assumed to be with the other, at her home. They had stopped worrying: one at least of the hazards of adolescence had not presented itself.

Eventually Joan would arrive home, greet her mother, and change out of her school uniform. Later there would be homework. Both parents were relieved that things seemed to be going smoothly with their only daughter.

But, several times a week, she spent an hour or two, not at Brenda's home, but with one of their teachers, in his flat. He liked the school uniforms of girls. He had taken charge of her sexuality, and seduced her.

"You know I don't like Bryan," said Brenda. "Because he's calculating, and you're not the first."

"I know I'm not the first. How could I be? But Bryan isn't calculating. He loves me, and I love him." It was, of course, the sacred word.

"Of course you do." Brenda would not press too hard. "I'm sure he does too."

They continued to walk, carrying their symbols of immaturity - their school satchels.

"What if you go to university, Joan?"

"I won't - unless it's London. I'll be living with him."

"Do they know?"

"No, of course not. I only put London on my form. I don't know where they think I'll be. At home, probably. They don't say anything, of course, just assume."

She paused.

"Oh, how I hate it all - parents, and family, all that."

Both knew it was not completely true.

"Has he asked you to live with him?"

"Of course he has."

"I won't say: 'what about his wife'. I know they're not living together."

It pained Brenda, close enough to Joan to be entitled to talk to her about Bryan, but detached enough to have a different view of him, that she thought him to be not only calculating, but evil. She was sure that Joan was one in a long series, and would be thrown aside. But the instinctive solidarity of one generation against another meant that she must connive in the deception necessary. She also envied Joan. Whatever the sequel, and the final effect upon her, she was, in the present, fully engaged in what everyone seemed to desire most - an absorbing, unequivocally physical, love affair. Perhaps, thought Brenda, she had been at exactly the right age for it: everyone else came to it too late.

Even Brenda was not told how it was to be thus engaged. 'He's fantastic!' Joan might say, but the word was devalued and there were none suitable. It was a kind of discretion that there were none, and it was a loyalty to her lover.

She had delighted in the experienced hands which had first stroked her under the school uniform, had patiently shown her her beauty, had filled her life with magic, and finally led her to unimaginable explosions of joy.

She could not understand how she had been able to conduct the rest of her life, and why no-one had noticed. They must have thought I was just being adolescent, she had concluded.

*

Each of the children had a room of his own: it had been one of the parents' assumptions that this was necessary for the full development of personality. They had watched as the children filled their rooms with souvenirs, and symbols - as they must assume - of their four personalities.

They were mistaken in their assumption. Edward, whose walls were hung with the contemporary symbols of his peers, lived a life quite different from theirs. The display of symbols in his room was ironic: his interests were otherwise.

At fourteen his mind was made up: the framework of his life was complete. He did not see what could be added beyond experience - and that must be arbitrary and random.

He knew the excitements of poetry, philosophy, music, and of idealism, and shared them with one school friend, Roy. They had educated themselves, and each other, sharing their discoveries as they came upon them.

At school they were thought eccentric, but not too much so: they were so detached from the interests of their schoolfellows, and of their teachers, that there was little ground for dispute. With the outer layers of their minds they handled the academic requirements of the school programme; with the outer layers of their personalities they handled their social relationships.

In the family, Edward's precocity was accommodated easily. It was to be expected that one of the children would be exceptional; it did not seem to have affected his nervous balance. The parents hoped that it would not interfere with his education, that he would succeed in climbing some approved ladder - at least for the time being. Then, they fully expected, he would take off on his own.

Edward and Roy had discovered, with excitement, the hypotheses of Chomsky.

"It's so obvious!" said Edward. "Why didn't we think of it?"

"I suppose," said Roy, "because we weren't thinking in that area."

"Even if we had been, would we have thought of it? And how many more areas are there we aren't thinking in? Just ordinary areas."

Sometimes they had worked out certainties, then, looking into the matter, had found that someone had done the same before them. Wittgenstein, they admitted, had scooped them. His area was one everyone thought about and it should have been easy.

"Surely we know enough about most areas to think of the obvious!"

"Think of a tiny insect hovering ... its wings going at enormous speed. All those signals to the brain and back, and much smaller than a pinhead. It should have been obvious, hundreds of years ago, that that meant an atomic theory of matter."

"It's like fighting your way out of a bag. It takes Newton, Darwin, or Freud, to get out of the bag ... to see that there is a bag!"

"I suppose the bag is whatever people happen to think at the time. You're surrounded by it."

The approved - the calculatedly controversial - subjects of their school debates amused but did not interest them. Either the questions were meaningless or the answers were obvious.

But in one area Edward was earthbound. Passionately aware of music, he had been determined to take part in it. He wanted to soar, personally, not at second-hand. He played the oboe, but found it hard. It seemed there were no short cuts: one had simply to master the eccentricities of the instrument, its absurd obstacles to smooth performance. Dogged, sore-lipped, afraid that he had no talent - was perhaps congenitally unable to play the oboe - he forced himself to learn its arbitrary rules and to develop, slowly, an elementary technique.

III

Madge and Joan were at home. The door-bell rang.

"It'll be Deirdre," said Madge. "She'll want to talk. Do take the children up to your room. I can't bear to see them soaking it all up. They want to hear it all the time."

Seeing Deirdre with her children, at the front door, Madge was reminded of her own phrase. The children did indeed look stricken, and just like little birds. They looked closely into her face, asking for sympathy, or admiration. Joan took them upstairs.

Deirdre did not wait. "I'm absolutely shattered," she said.

Madge tried to soothe her, to bring her further into the house. Perhaps they would have a cup of tea.

"We've just heard *he's* petitioning! It's he who walked out, he has all the money, he has the girlfriend, and he's bringing *me* to court!"

Madge said nothing.

"And it's not even the first time." Deirdre stopped, as though wondering whether to admit Madge into further confidences.

"You remember our *au pair* girl? The one who left suddenly ... and before that. There's no use pretending any more ..."

"But Deirdre, why don't you just tell me what's happening?"

"He never told me how much money we had. And now it turns out he had *two* accounts. God knows what was in the other. Since the ... break-up, he won't discuss it. '*Sod off*', he said, when I rang."

"Would you believe it," she went on. "Sod off! We *both* saw a psychiatrist, you know. There's no doubt where *he* stood. 'Mrs Wood', he said, 'you'll just have to stand up for yourself. Otherwise he'll walk all over you'. I asked him if he'd told *him* that. He said he had, of course."

She breathed heavily, as though to raise steam.

"Do you know, I couldn't even pay the laundry bill without asking him. I can't think how I put up with it. Meanness ... years and years ..."

"But Deirdre," said Madge, "you told me that you wanted him

back."

"Of course I want him back."

Madge remained quiet.

"That's what I want to talk to you about."

She stopped.

"Will you do something for me, Madge?" she said suddenly. "Just tell Tom, or ask Martin to tell him ... just say if he comes back it'll be different."

"But Deirdre, you'll have to tell me more than that."

"Well ... I'm surprised you didn't know. I'm surprised you didn't hear it all through the wall, as a matter of fact. We did rather go at each other before he ... went."

"It's a very thick wall, Deirdre."

"It went on for days, actually. Just tell him I've seen the point, and he'll come back."

Madge felt bound, at last, to give an opinion. "I don't think he will, Deirdre. It must have been ... very hard for him to walk out. Everyone knows it now. He'd be a fool ... it would be another ordeal ... for him to come back."

Deirdre looked downcast. "Of course, we tried to keep it quiet. I thought he'd be back before people got to know."

It was true, up to a point, thought Madge, that they had tried to keep it quiet. At least, those who had not heard, were not told. But as soon as they *had* heard, had been admitted into the circle of those who knew, they were engulfed in it - in telephoned opinions, prognostications, and up-to-date versions.

"And there *is* Marjorie," said Madge. "He won't drop her like that. He may be quite satisfied with things as they are."

"She won't drop him, more like," said Deirdre. "Now she's got her claws in."

"Of course, he must be missing the children."

"What's she got that I haven't got? After all, let's face it, she's no chicken ... Come to that, it's not as though he's any Don Juan. I could tell you a few things ..."

Madge hoped that she would not do so.

"It won't last long. She'll soon find out ... Do you know, he doesn't even bother about their birthdays. You'd think, with his income, he'd be above that sort of meanness."

Again Deirdre seemed to need to raise steam.

"You go along for years, thinking everything's fine, putting all you can into it, and then suddenly one day ... off he goes!"

She paused.

"It's just too funny! Text-book stuff, really. I ought to have been ready for it. Male menopause, they call it."

"What have you got on today?" asked Madge. "Is it your solicitor?"

"I should say so. He'll see what's coming to him. When we finish with him he'll be glad to *crawl* back. He's not getting away with it."

"But isn't it all expensive? I've always heard people should keep away from the law as long as they can."

"Expensive! He can afford it."

*

"Hello, Tom," said Martin. "Nice to see you." They had met in a pub.

"Hello, Martin. It is nice to see you."

They looked around for a table, and bought drinks.

"I don't want to talk about this ... business, Martin. I'm afraid I'm becoming a bore about it." He sounded exasperated, perhaps defiant, but also anxious, worn, and guilty.

"Anyone would think I *was* the guilty party, the way Deirdre goes on. From what I've heard, I'm the blackest devil who ever left the matrimonial home."

Martin waited, but said nothing.

"There comes a point, Martin, when the relief of doing it is overwhelming. I tell you, when I finally decided, I felt - for a few hours at least - positively happy. Of course, everything's descended on me since."

"Everything, Tom! But surely ..."

"I do believe I'd have walked out when I did even if Marjorie hadn't existed. But there's no doubt, one does need to have somewhere to go."

Tom seemed to be thoughtful.

"What Deirdre doesn't seem to realise is ... one is bound to have problems ... *at the other end*!"

Martin raised an eyebrow.

"Of course," Tom went on, "Marjorie's absolutely marvellous. But, you know, it's bound to be a bit ... awkward ... for her. People do know her around here. If I'm the guilty party, then she is too. And so far, Deirdre's digging in her heels. She'll wring out the last ounce. She absolutely *stages* incidents to show me up."

"I suppose," said Martin soberly, "the fact is, this is too small a community. You know, we all really live in a village. All the traffic of London flows through twice a day, but it's still a village."

"Do you know, the week after I ... moved out, it was Deb's birthday party. She's ten. We'd arranged it weeks before. I rang up and said I'd come anyway. We had a row, naturally ... When I got there, the house was empty. No-one there! God knows what she told them."

He too seemed, occasionally, to need to raise steam.

"She's absolutely *neurotic* about money. It's the only thing she'll talk about ... I ring up, to ask about the kids, and all she'll say is what bills have come in. And can she have more money. It's not as if I'm rolling in it!"

Tom had been speaking as though to himself. He turned to Martin. "Shall I tell you what finally decided me, Martin? I suddenly realised I didn't have any possessions of my own at all. I haven't got a ... study ... and I do have to take work home. I don't know how it happened. Somehow or other, we only had family possessions ... furniture, and that sort of thing. I hadn't even got a pipe! I used to smoke one, but she didn't like the smell, and eventually I gave it up."

He seemed exasperated by the pettiness of what he described.

"Of course, that's not important. It was probably good for me to give it up. But, you know ..."

Tom took a pipe from his pocket, and looked at it.

"Well, Tom. I see you've got your pipe now," said Martin kindly.

Tom fumbled in his pockets; laboriously, and angrily, he tried to light his pipe, piling frustration upon rage.

"Of course," he said, "we're very cramped in Marjorie's flat."
He drew on his pipe.

"Another thing ... you see, what Deirdre's trying to do is to make it impossible to discuss anything rationally. Then she tells everyone what she wants them to think. I'm sure the telephone wires are red hot! And of course, *I* pay the bill. Do you know, she even tells people what the psychiatrist said about *me*!"

"Psychiatrist!"

"Well, you know, we both went to a sort of ... marriage expert. I thought everyone knew about it."

"I didn't know, Tom ..."

"It wasn't a success. After a bit he as good as told me she was a hopeless case. You know, if I wasn't willing to knuckle under ... You won't believe it, but even when I did smoke a pipe she wanted to choose it for me. Seriously, we'd go together to the shop ..."

He stopped, and both were quiet.

"How do the children seem to you, Martin?"

"I really haven't seen them, Tom. I believe Madge does sometimes ..."

"If I go to see the children, she makes a scene. And of course she won't let them come and see me ..."

"But surely, you'll get all that sorted out eventually?"

"She won't shift on anything. That means five years. My chap says I ought to go to court, or force her to by cutting off the money ... or something like that."

Tom looked at Martin anxiously. "I'm not asking for advice, Martin. I just value talking to you - as a friend. As a matter of fact I'd love you ... and Madge ... to come and see us. We haven't much of a place to entertain anyone, but ..."

"Of course, we'd ..."

Tom interrupted again. "You've no idea how sordid it can be. When everything is calculated against you. I left quite a few things behind I really need. My dinner jacket, for instance. But just to go and get it will be an ordeal. She'll have changed the locks by now. She'll make it look as though I'm raiding the family home, or something. The kids will be there, watching."

Again he drew on his pipe.

"Or that miserable travelling bag. I need it. But naturally, I don't know *whose* it is. *We* bought it. So it's an issue. She'll fight over it, or leave it on the pavement outside the house, or something equally mad. She just won't discuss anything rationally. It's not as though she's badly off. She has her own money - a legacy I didn't know anything about. She's so damned mean ... It's not even ..." Tom stopped, as though uncertain whether to go on.

"She can't pretend," he said, after some moments, "that she's innocent herself."

Martin waited, but Tom did not explain what he had meant.

"It's not a question of innocence or guilt, surely," said Martin.

"No, I mean," said Tom, "that *she* hasn't been above an affair or two. Of course, now that I've actually gone off with Marjorie, that's all forgotten."

He changed direction abruptly. "She even argues about the car! She's never driven it - never passed her test. And I need it. But she says it's ours, not mine!"

It seemed to Martin that Tom's need was for reassurance about his conduct, not about his prospects. But he did not tread on that ground. "Well," he said, "things do get sorted out, you know. Hard going, sometimes, but sorted out, in the end."

Tom did not seem to be reassured. "There's nothing so awful as the breakdown of a marriage, Martin. You're so lucky. With Madge, I mean."

"I have enjoyed our chat," he went on. "Do keep in touch."

"Of course," said Martin. "I'd like to."

*

Martin and Madge had met Jim and Alice in a pub. In their society this was a sign of a superior friendship. Neither couple were hosts, there was nothing to be reciprocated; they had met for their mutual pleasure. Martin and Madge had suggested the meeting.

"It's lovely to see you," said Alice. "I know you're anxious about us. And we're not very good company at present."

"Of course you are," said Martin. "And we mustn't keep off

the subject of your horrible crack. We do want to know how it's all going."

"I'll tell you one thing," said Jim. "I won't be writing a play about a couple, with a crack in their house, and a crack in their marriage."

Alice smiled and reached toward him.

"Unless, of course, I think of another twist."

"The fact is," said Alice, "although we're both upset, of course ... no, we're desperate sometimes ... it hasn't really anything to do with *us*. Neither of us built the house, neither talked the other into buying it. It's just a ... problem we have to sort out."

"How *is* it going?" said Martin.

"Our side are waiting for counsel's opinion," said Alice.

"Oh dear! That!"

Alice looked at Martin with enquiry. "You can't sue him if he gets it wrong," he said.

"Have you noticed," he went on, "that the most highly paid professions - the law, and medicine - are those people need to call on when they're most desperate? When, you might imagine, the ... *need* was the most important thing."

"Don't forget bankers," said Jim. "You might imagine that as their job is to protect your money they'd make sure none of it went astray. But somehow ... they get rich."

"All very much in our thinking at present," said Alice.

Madge spoke gently, anxious again for her friends. "Why is medicine in your thinking? I know about the others, of course."

"We want children," said Alice. "Something's wrong, and I'm getting on a bit."

All became silent. "We sometimes think we want four, like you," she went on. "In spite of the state of the world. At least, when we look at yours - and you - we want four."

"I expect we'll settle for two," said Jim. "It'll be our gesture to the state of the world."

"Our gesture is to have you as friends," said Martin. "You're a lot younger than we are. We can't really talk to our kids. But we seem to talk to you, and it tells us something about them - and the state of the world."

"It's not age," said Jim. "It's the parent-child thing. No-one can talk to his children - or parents. We're all too clogged up. And as for the generations, they're turning over every ten years nowadays. Ours will be ... unthinkable."

"And yet," said Alice, "we do seem to want them."

"It's because," said Jim, "*they*, at least, come absolutely unpolluted."

"Does anyone *really* think about the state of the world?" said Madge. "Of course, we *worry*, and we look at the news. But what we actually do is ... just carry on with our own things."

"It's one of my problems," said Jim. "My plays, if possible, have to be - or seem to be - in the 80s. But who really knows about them? That's why, if we can get away with it, we write about the last century - or the stone age. Or we fake it, by looking at other plays."

"He's too serious about it," said Alice.

"It's not that at all," said Jim. "I know nothing changes, but I have to pretend it does."

He sighed, and went on. "I really ought to have a proper job. You know - go to the office every day, have business lunches ... that sort of thing."

"You do have an office, Jim."

"Not really, Alice. Just a desk."

"It's I who ought to have a proper job," said Alice. "Instead of staying at home, painting pictures no-one wants."

"People do want them, Alice."

"Just a few. I couldn't make a living. I don't have to, of course, but it isn't fair to you."

"Why isn't it fair to me?"

"Because, my darling, I can indulge in absolute integrity, which no-one cares about, and you have to bend yours, to support us."

"That's not how I see it." Jim turned, to bring Martin and Madge into the conversation. "The real trouble is, what I do is just too hard for me. I have an idea - I always think it's a great idea - but by the time I've worked out how to do it, I'm bored, or exhausted."

He grimaced, then went on. "For example: you know how everyone says, at a party, 'did you have any trouble getting here?'

They don't want an answer, of course; it's like saying something about the weather. But now, it could be a real question. People *could* have trouble getting wherever they want to go. You might drive through a riot, or you might be mugged. That's an 80s theme, if you like. Well, in my ... notional play, the characters really talk about it, but only, like the weather, as an inconvenience - an accepted part of life. Just conversation starters. One character describes proudly how he has a car with sliding doors. It fits exactly into his garage, with no room to spare on either side. He opens the garage door by remote control when he arrives home. He can see there's no intruder in the garage, no-one can get in behind him, and when he drives his car in, the door into the house is exactly opposite the sliding door of his car. And so on - you know, they compare notes about their security devices, then go on to talk about other things, like the latest Glyndebourne production."

"Our house isn't too well placed," said Alice. "We don't like to admit it, but it sometimes seems crazy to go through the ... ordeal of having it repaired, and then, what have we got - just a funny looking house where we don't particularly want to be. And yet, it looked great when we bought it. You know, positively adventurous."

"What else can we do?" said Jim. "We can't move. No-one will buy it until it's repaired. We have a mortgage, of course, a big one. That seemed adventurous, too." Madge sensed a tension between them again, as she had done at the party. But she could not tell whether there was a disagreement, or if there was, on which side either stood.

"We're in that play too," said Martin. "A little further away, of course. Being older, we think that's how it should be. We just hope it won't move our way."

"Perhaps, being older," said Madge, "we think we mightn't be there if it does."

"That's very sad, Madge," said Jim. He made a small gesture, signifying affection, denying that she was older.

"We're really talking about Brixton, aren't we?" said Martin. "We live about three miles from it, and you about two miles. 'White liberals' as we are, we all wish it wasn't just there."

"Why, Martin?" said Alice.

"She knows why," said Jim. "She means say it for us."

"Guilts, helplessnesses, and fears, Alice. Just some of the things we can't talk to kids about."

"Why not?"

"Well, Alice, would you?"

"We liked going to Sussex," Martin went on. "It seemed harmless, and thoroughly deserved. We sometimes went to Brighton. When the gangs started to fight on the beach and promenade we didn't worry too much, just made sure we didn't go at weekends. Then we began to realise we'd always passed through Brixton. We still do. We never stopped, of course. Now it's the symbol - the visible distillation - of everything that's wrong."

"Except for the bomb, of course," said Madge.

"So it's the fire next time, either way," said Jim.

"The whole point about a house," said Alice, "is that you should feel safe in it. That you can come in from the dangerous, big world, and there, at least, your own small world is all right." Consciously, and deliberately, she had narrowed her vision.

"If you haven't got that, can't even cultivate your own rotten garden ..."

"Don't we all actually think," said Martin, "that somehow or other, we personally will survive? But will the kids? I do sometimes have fears that one of them will be run over, or beaten up, or raped. *That's* the unthinkable. Never mind the bomb."

The others said nothing. Martin saw that he had silenced them: he had expressed the theme of their conversation in real terms.

"Don't forget most murders are committed in the family," said Jim, cheerfully.

"That is cheering, Jim. That's one thing that's probably not getting any worse."

"It's time we had another round," said Jim. He saw to it.

"Why don't you write that, Jim?" said Martin later. "You might have your 80s play."

"I might, but then again, no-one might notice. I've told you the point of my play in two minutes. Less. How could I bear to work on it for weeks - months? And honestly, I have one a day - one idea which could be a play. Sometimes it's just a title."

He thought for a moment. " 'Ways of talking to your wife'. What do you think of that?" He, too, had narrowed his vision.

"It's a good title," said Martin.

Jim sighed. "Let me tell you some of them: some people pretend they're talking to the children, or to the pets; some go to the marriage guidance expert, and talk to him. Some just write books at each other. And here's another: 'are we watching TV, or is TV watching us?' "

"Jim, please write that one," said Alice.

"There's another thing. I always start by wanting to say something. So I invent characters. Then, painfully - and lengthily - I make them speak and act. I watch and listen to people to help me to do it. It's my trade. But then I hear two minutes of conversation which is actually *better*! Today I saw two men walking together. One said, very purposefully, but as far as I could tell not bitterly: 'all right, let's go and buy *two* sponges'. They crossed the road and went into Woolworths. A few minutes later they came out and went into Boots. The trouble is, it's all there already. A two-minute play!"

"Then the other day," he went on, "I heard three men in a pub. One said: 'actually, I'm married, you know'. The second said: 'so am I, apparently'. Then the third said: 'well, so am I, basically'."

All laughed.

"Of course, I *want* to write plays. I have the absurd idea - we all do - that as soon as people see my play they'll change their ways."

"What about us?" said Madge. "You know us well. Don't we give you any ideas?"

Jim pretended to think. They saw that he would tease them. "We do know you very well. But I don't think I could afford to put you in a play."

"Why not, Jim?"

"We love you both. But you're too quiet. And you're 60s people. My agent wouldn't wear it for a minute."

*

Meeting in a corridor, Martin and Tony Booth both stopped.

"Oh, I say. Just a word ..." said Tony.

They went into Martin's room. Tony seemed to be embarrassed. For a coming top man, thought Martin, he's easily embarrassed.

"We did enjoy your party, you know."

"We enjoyed it too, Tony. We liked your wife very much."

"Elizabeth will be writing to ... Madge ..."

"Oh no! Please tell her not to. It's really very sweet of her but ..."

"Well ... we must, some time ... Elizabeth and I must ..."

"Of course, we'd love to ..."

Tony took a cigarette case from his pocket.

"Do you ...?"

"No, luckily. I never started."

"Very wise. Now *I'm* a complete addict. Used to be forty a day. Cut it down to twenty for a time. But I'm back to thirty now."

"It's too many," said Martin, "for a scientist who uses statistics."

"Yes, I know that ..."

Both were silent. How odd, thought Martin, that I'm taking pills - perhaps they're to help me cope with him - and he smokes thirty cigarettes a day - to help him cope with me, I expect.

"Have you ever tried a pipe, Tony?"

"Yes, I tried it once. Not fast enough for me, I'm afraid."

"You do know that it's ... that pipe-smoking is relatively safe, don't you?"

"Oh yes, I do. Of course I wish I could give it up. It's expensive, as well as dangerous. But ... I just have to hope I'm in the wings of the statistics."

They were silent again. "Your car all right now?" said Martin.

"Yes thanks. Why? Did I tell you about it?"

"You did tell me you were having trouble with a garage."

"Well yes, I was. They admitted in the end they'd never handled the make before. When I wouldn't pay they cut up rough at first. But my solicitor wrote, and they caved in. Shouldn't have used them in the first place, of course, but they were handy."

"What was it, actually, Tony?"

"Centrifugal oil pump. Absolutely bunged up. Simply wasn't passing any oil. Could have been worse, of course: could have ruined my engine."

"Always best to stick to someone who knows your car. Especially if it's a bit exotic."

Tony had finished his cigarette.

"Do let's have a chat, soon," Martin went on. "I'd like to know how you feel about things. How ... things are working out."

"Yes, I'd like to ... very much."

Tony looked at his watch, then went on. "Must rush now. We must have a natter, some time. Sooner rather than later, eh?"

2

IV

"Oh Martin, how did you know? I *longed* to see you!"

"Liz, is today all right?"

"He's away. Come in."

"I won't come in. Can we go out?" They stood at a kitchen door: it led to a back garden. Martin had walked through the garden from a back gate. The house, large and expensive, stood at the edge of Ashdown Forest. There was a double garage with its door open, and one car in it.

"It's a *lovely* day," she said. "Go to our place. I'll bring food and drink. I'll be there in twenty minutes."

She reached out her hand; he grasped it through the open, upper half of the door.

"How marvellous to see you!" she went on. "Go on, I can't wait to talk to you."

In a clearing in the forest, as he waited for her, he wondered why he had not rung before coming. There had been wasted journeys. He had, once or twice, driven back to London without seeing her. But today, surprised by a sudden need, he had wanted her to be surprised too.

When she came, they kissed and embraced. "You're such a waif," he said. "There's nothing to you." She smiled into his shoulder.

"I've a bottle of wine, and a Thermos of coffee."

They found a spot; he put a rug on the ground.

"Of course, I know why you wouldn't come in," she went on. "But it isn't his house. It's mine too. I know this forest is ours, darling Martin, but it's sometimes cold, and sometimes wet. Not today, fortunately. Anyhow, I'm so glad to see you. I was so unhappy today."

"About Helen?"

"It's so silly. I hated seeing her off. I know it's only for a few weeks. I expect she'll enjoy herself. But when she puts on her brave look ... her nose goes a little pale ... oh dear! I think I'm getting too old to bear unhappiness - at least to do with children."

"I know. One can bear one's own, but not one's children's."

"I used to be glad when I found I could bear some unhappiness. One never knows how bad anything's going to be ... or whether one will be able to bear it. It all comes from within."

"But Liz, one never knows how *good* anything's going to be."

"You mean us, don't you, Martin. Of course, it's only with you I experience it - have ever experienced it."

Kneeling on the ground, setting out what she had brought, she leant against him for a moment.

"Poor Helen. I don't think she experiences much. Not much joy, anyhow. It's my fault. We should have had another. It put too much responsibility on her, making her an only child."

"You can't be sure, Liz."

"It affected her, I'm sure. I don't know what to do about it."

"You can't do anything about it. It's too late. You can't even be sure it was your fault in the first place. Except for your genes, of course."

"Pour us some wine, Martin."

She looked at him curiously. "You've told me before," she said, "... that you can't really do anything about children. Have you been brooding about it?"

"No, Liz. But it's hard to accept. One worries that what one is doing to them may be exactly wrong. Hoping of course that it's exactly right. And all the time they're just going along, practically ready-made, just putting up with you and waiting to be let out."

"You are pessimistic today, Martin. But how do you know? How do you know they're ready-made?"

"Well, as a matter of fact, there were moments when I realised that my children's characters *were* already formed - two of them anyway - beyond anyone's capacity to change them."

"And obviously," he went on, "formed some time before that. God knows how! I suddenly realised, when Robert was seven or eight, that he was listening hard when anyone talked about him, and pretending not to. He was a handsome little boy: people often talked about him - old ladies in boarding houses. Naturally, from then on I tried not to let anyone do it - as though avoiding the symptom could change anything."

"But now," he seemed to speak a little bitterly, "you can see self-absorption in everything he does."

"Not everything, surely! From what you've told me, he must be really very nice, and very charming."

"Of course he is. All my children are nice ... and charming. But with Robert, he clears the ground first, makes sure everything's in order for him."

"You're too hard on him, Martin."

"Madge and I didn't talk about it much, but we accommodated to it. We tried to avoid coming to that point. But sometimes we all misjudged it. He wanted something quite unreasonable, or we dug in our heels, unreasonably, before he'd done whatever we were expecting."

"You are hard on them, Martin. And yet you do seem to love them. As a matter of fact you seem to be obsessed by them. I've never met a parent like you before."

"We're all the same. Madge is just as bad. You can't help it. At first you're listening to make sure they're not falling out of their cots. Then you hover around to see they don't catch their fingers in doors - or bicycle chains. Eventually you just want to know they're all right, without actually asking. And ... things being as they are, there's no guarantee that they will be. That's twenty or thirty years ..."

"But surely *he'll* be all right," she said. "From what you say, it seems to me he'll see to it. Anyway, what do you mean by 'all right'?"

"I suppose I mean ... happy. Or at least fulfilled in some way."

He stopped and thought for a moment. "I don't even entirely like them. Of course I love them - whatever that means - but I don't especially want to see them."

"You're not fair to yourself, Martin."

"I suppose ... I suppose if I felt sure about the other thing, felt sure he wouldn't expose enormities of character, I'd like to see more of Robert. For pleasure, I mean. Not just to reassure myself what a good father I'd been."

"Can you separate it all?"

Now he looked at her curiously.

"I've just thought again. Why am I talking to you about my children? I've done it a lot."

"Why not? I'm fascinated by them too. Because they're yours, I suppose. And I've only Helen. Not even nephews or nieces ... as close as yours."

"You're very generous not to resent them."

"Why should I? They're you! We've accepted that ... this ... is quite separate. You have your family, Madge ... even your job. I have Helen ... and him, I suppose."

"You are the generous one, as a matter of fact," she went on. "You give me so much; how could I complain?"

He wondered how long she would be persuaded of it.

"What are you thinking?" she said.

"I'm asking myself," he said, "how long it will be before you do resent my family. And telling myself to be careful not to give you too much cause. Like asking you to choose a present for Madge. It's been done, you know."

She smiled, and leant against him again.

"Or perhaps worse, for one of the children. After all, we were very determined about it, having four."

"I don't resent them at all, Martin. Why should I? And I do notice that you never criticise Madge. It's very grown-up of you."

"Why should I criticise her? She's a nice woman. She's stuck with me just as much as I am with her. She's getting older, and hates it, and she hates the family getting smaller. Sometimes I feel, not only guilty ... because of us, but just sorry for her."

Abruptly, he changed his mood. "Come to that, I'm stuck with you! And I haven't even reached double figures."

She followed him. "I'm jealous of those others, Martin. I don't mean Madge. I mean before her. Even if I hadn't met you, how dare you be unfaithful to me!"

"I'm sorry. How was I to know?"

"You should have waited. Anyway, double figures! And I've only had two. And so different ..."

"Talk about it, Martin," she went on. "Why are you stuck with me?"

He knew that she knew the answer, and wanted only to hear it.

"It's the 'tingle' when I think about you. It came at the beginning. When it didn't fade in a week I knew I was falling in love with you. It still comes when I know I'm going to see you."

"As much as before?"

"Nearly. Except, of course, when I hate you. Then it doesn't come for a time. As soon as I forgive you it starts again."

"And what about John? When was his character revealed?"

He detected the slight irony in the world. By ignoring it he would cancel it. But he did not seem to want to speak about John.

"It was a silly little thing of giving presents. He surprised us all one day by buying things - one for each of us. He may have saved up ... but we think he probably took the money - from Madge's bag. We were shocked, after our careful ... 'progressive' efforts, that he could be insecure. Naturally, we redoubled them. Of course we didn't ask where he'd got the money. And he still wants to be reassured. He tries not to let us see it, of course."

Again he seemed to speak bitterly, but mocking himself. "Where did we go wrong?"

"Well, Martin, surely *he's* extremely nice and charming."

"Of course he is. I didn't say he wasn't. Anyhow, we see so little of him. He's always away somewhere."

"Martin, you're too severe on them. Surely families aren't really so problematical. We've talked about them before. I just think you're tired."

"Families are problematical, Liz. Hell sometimes. We did somehow float through and it slowly got better. Of course only Joan and Edward are left: Joan seems to have settled down ... and Edward, well, he hasn't really erupted yet. Probably when he does we'll be so experienced ..."

"And what about Joan? Surely *she's* a complete sweetie!"

"I only said two moments of revelation. I don't really know about Joan. She's very warm ... and outgiving. Seems to feel responsible for us all. But she's a bit of a mystery - to Madge as well, I think. Of course, she's only seventeen: perhaps she hasn't shown her true colours yet. On the whole, I quite like her."

"You adore her!"

"She's very beautiful - those dark eyes, and hair - but really extraordinary. Surely no more sexy costume has ever been devised than a school uniform. But she can't bear it. It's obviously more important to look a bit older ... than sexy."

"I wish I knew them. But of course I can't. I wish I could just see them."

"At least she had all the advantages. Two big brothers - reasonably adoring, or at least tolerating. And one little brother. No reason why she shouldn't be utterly normal. I expect she is. She certainly wanted to marry me at the right time, and hated Madge at the right time. But she used to have rages ... which we simply decided to forget."

So did Madge, he thought suddenly.

"And she had mysterious bouts of crying." He looked sad, as though himself about to weep. "Not now. She's pretty cool now."

He still looked sad. "Did I tell you this? Once she'd had a row with Madge and gone out when Madge had told her not to. I was up late. Madge had gone to bed. When she came in she didn't say anything, just pointed to her eyes. As though to say 'don't spoil it'."

"Did you?"

"Of course not, Liz."

"I honestly don't know," he went on, "how anyone dares have children. As I said, you can't really do anything about them. I'm still astonished that mine are so different from each other. Robert - sharp but quite unintellectual, nasty sometimes, extrovert, fun; and Edward ... apparently just the opposite."

"What about Edward?"

Martin thought for a moment. "I suppose we didn't take so much notice, after the first two. Probably good for them. He's confident, I think. Quiet, of course, but very bright when he brings himself to say anything."

It was not the whole of what he thought. On the contrary, he had always felt that a part of his own fragility was lodged in Edward. Panic fears about his children - that one of them might be killed in an accident, or die of some rare disease - always referred to

Edward. He remembered a happening, some years before, about which he had not told Liz. It was near the start of their affair and he was tormented by guilt: he feared what he might do to his children. On a day when he was to see her he had driven Edward to school. He was ten, and obsessively involved with a model which he had made at home to a pattern given him at school. The day had come for all the models to be brought to school and shown.

Martin had watched him cross the road and enter the school gate; he prepared to drive off. Suddenly Edward turned and came back to the edge of the pavement, almost running. He stopped and stood poised: there was terror in his eyes. At the same moment Martin realised that both had forgotten about the model, which lay on the back seat. It seemed that Edward might run into the road, into the busy traffic. Martin threw open the door of his car and shouted desperately.

"There's one thing, Liz. They always close ranks in company. That's why, I suppose, everyone thinks they're charming. It is nice of them: we both appreciate it. As a matter of fact, when it's about them, we seem to agree about most things."

"You are, actually, a close family, aren't you, Martin."

"I suppose we are." He seemed surprised.

"As you know, the regret I have is having only one. But it isn't your fault. You were a bit late on the scene for me to blame you."

"Well, my four rather absorbed my paternal instinct." He looked at his watch.

"Don't do that, Martin."

"It's all cricket bats ... cat baskets ... orange juice ... remedial shoes ... Guy Fawkes ... teenage parties ..."

"You loved it!"

"I wonder."

"I'm not really much use to you, Liz. I don't take you away from your husband. I don't see you too often. I just come, I don't even say when I'm coming ... and then I pour out my woes."

"Well, you haven't been doing that. Why ... how is it all?"

"The usual sort of thing. I don't know why I get so involved. After all, it's only academic politics. In twenty ... no, five years' time, no-one will care about it."

She smiled. "I'm sure they will, Martin."

"No, Liz. I don't think anyone will even know it happened. If we win, then a few hundred students will be slightly better educated than if we don't. Or they'll have the chance to be. But in five years' time something else will have changed it all. There'll be some new policy, and my little reform will be swept away."

"You shouldn't get so involved, Martin. Not because it isn't important: it obviously is important. But I think you get too emotionally involved."

"I know that, Liz. But the only other person who knows is you."

He paused.

"That's really the point. It's just because, in the argument itself, among my stupid colleagues, I can't afford to show that it's important to me. It would weaken my position. I have to let facts speak for themselves ... or at least pretend that's what I'm doing. As though I don't really care too much. As a matter of fact, I'm not really any good at that sort of thing."

"I know that's hard for you, Martin."

"Some of my colleagues wouldn't be above opposing me just because they saw I was emotionally involved. So there I am, hour after hour, afternoon after afternoon, being Dean, giving everyone a fair chance, trying to ignore the stupidities of some of them, trying to drag it along the way I want ... steering it between the different groups, so that at least *something* will happen."

"It's pretending not to be stressed," he went on, "that is the stress. I can *feel* ... whatever it is - adrenalin, blood or acid ..."

He was quiet for some moments.

"I suppose the trouble is that I'm no longer one thing or the other. I'm obviously not bright and up-and-coming - to be feared on that account. And I'm not one of the knights, looking in from more important meetings elsewhere - but only to make sure nothing gets away from them - and to be feared on that account. I'm just there in the middle, holding what I consider to be my baby, and stuck with it."

"But isn't everyone in the same boat really? I bet the up-and-coming, even the knights, think they're neither one thing nor the other."

He thought about her question. "It could be, Liz. But I can't help feeling I enjoyed the up-and-coming part more. And if I did happen to be one of the ... great, I think I'd enjoy that too. There's even the nagging doubt about wasting all this time being Dean. It sounds important, but perhaps I'm only someone else's clerk - I'm not sure whose. The up-and-coming are catching me up, and the great are getting still further away."

"I used to enjoy the thing itself," he went on. "I can't quite understand how that got submerged in all this ... calculation."

"But surely this ... battle of yours is about the thing itself."

"Yes, that's true. It's about it, but it's not *it*. Of course, there's another nagging doubt: that I'm only doing it to keep away from the thing itself - which I'm not so good at ... or even interested in ... as I was."

"I told you that you're not fair to yourself," she said. "And as for being no use to me, as you said at the beginning, I think it's absolutely marvellous that you do come. I *love* it. I even love to hear about your ... academic politics. Because it is you, in there ... in that battle, whatever it is. I don't know exactly what it's about, but I'm sure I'd think you were right."

"I shouldn't waste time on it, when I'm with you."

"What about that new professor of yours?"

He did not seem to want to answer. "Oh ... he's a pest sometimes. I expect I'll handle him."

He looked at his watch again. "I wonder," he said "if my family are under-sexed."

"But I thought they had girlfriends - and doesn't Joan have a boyfriend?"

"I was thinking about Madge, actually. We rather drifted into pyjamas, going to bed when each of us felt like it. And having separate baths."

"And beds, Martin?"

He seemed to have to dig into his memory. "Yes, we drifted into that too. We kept the double bed, of course, but had a single bed as well. I hardly remember why ... probably because I often worked late."

"Eventually," he went on, "she seemed always to be in the middle of the double bed, and asleep, when I got there."

"That's funny, Martin. It rings a bell."

"When you turned up, of course, I suppose I was glad."

"I hope." Martin went on, "she's reasonably contented. After all, she's still only about forty-eight. She enjoys the family, I think - even though it's dissolving, and she enjoys her classes."

"As I said, Martin, you never say anything unkind about her."

"I was *glad*, Liz."

He seemed glad to leave the subject.

"As for the girlfriends, it's true they have them. But it doesn't seem all that intense. Not at all what I remember - more like the tennis club than you'd expect. Why, John actually belongs to one! I thought that sort of thing was going out."

"Not around here, Martin."

"I suppose we're lucky we had three boys. One doesn't worry so much about them. And when they bring their girlfriends, if we don't happen to like them, we only have to wait, and they'll have new ones."

"What about Joan?"

"Oh, she has boyfriends. I've seen a few of them: they're a bit awkward, but very nice. She seems to be sensible about it all; keeps it in proportion. They all do."

"*Can* it be kept in proportion, Martin? Did you? Did we?"

He tried to remember, and both were quiet for a time.

"Oddly enough," she said, "... I mean, it's a little odd, in the circumstances, but what I actually need most is faithfulness. And fortunately, you are faithful to me."

"I really couldn't keep two going ..." he began, teasing her.

"No, Martin. You really are. I know I'm the one you relax with. And even though we don't too often get to bed together, I know you wouldn't with anyone else."

"Go to bed, you mean?"

"No, Martin. Relax."

They had nearly finished the wine. She now looked at him anxiously.

"There's one thing I didn't say."

He saw the change in her mood. "Oh Liz! About the hospital. Of course. I should have asked."

"I didn't want to say before. I had my appointment."

"Oh!" He touched her arm.

"What happened?"

"I've been longing to tell you. And not wanting to. They want me to go in ..."

"Oh no!"

"For 'observation'. Shall I go? I want you to say." Now she spoke desperately. It was some moments before he could reply.

"If it were anyone else of course I'd say 'yes' at once. It's the only thing to do. It would be stupid not to. But you or I ... *I'd* probably go on, refusing to admit there was anything wrong with me. I'd think that being in hospital, having tests, would be to admit I was ill ... would be to *be* ill."

Now she reached out a hand and touched him.

"Even one of the children," he went on. "I'd have no doubt what to do. But you!"

"But Martin, when you make a decision for yourself you know you can change your mind, so you have to keep up your decision. That makes it harder. If you tell me what to do I'll do it. I want *you* to say. There's no-one else I would ask."

She paused.

"There's no-one else I *can* ask."

"Oh ..." He looked at the ground. "But Liz ... couldn't you ask him? After all, he is a doctor. Surely he could help you."

"He's not that sort, Martin."

"I know he isn't. But he knows people. He could put you on to someone."

"It's not fair," she said suddenly. "I shouldn't make you say. Let's not talk about it."

"Of course you should go, Liz."

"Let's talk about it another time."

Now he spoke a little desperately. "When must you decide?"

"He said I shouldn't leave it too long."

Both wished that the subject of their conversation could be changed - that the afternoon, at least, could be saved. Quickly she moved behind him and put her arms around his neck as though to trap him, and so that she need not look at him.

"Do you remember when we first came here?" she said. "Do you remember exactly?"

"Of course!" He turned to her. "I remember everything. I did this."

He extricated one arm and traced the neck-line of her dress with a finger.

"Yes. It was sudden, and I didn't expect it."

He did it again, contemplatively. "And you said: 'you have the most adorable hands'!"

"Snob! You shouldn't remember that."

She paused.

"And you said: 'in that case, I suppose I score one'."

"Pig!" he said. "You shouldn't remember that."

He paused.

"And do you remember the time after that? You wore the same dress."

"Of course, Martin."

"That was bold, and very moving."

"I remember exactly," she said. "Afterwards you walked round and round. I felt very virginal, as a matter of fact."

She disengaged herself. He looked at his watch.

"Not yet, please, Martin!" She wanted to keep them there. "That was the time I said I was rather obsessional. And you said: 'then I'll have to make sure I'm the obsession'."

"It *is* time to go, I think, Liz."

She was unwilling. "I was telling a friend," she said, "that we are mentally as well as physically intimate. She didn't seem to understand. I meant ... that as well as everything else ... we have a sort of mental play: one moment sharp, another moment warm."

"I think it's you who supply them both."

"Nonsense!"

She paused, and put her arms around his neck again.

"Then you said 'Hooray'!"

"What a memory!"

Both smiled.

"I'll just clear everything up," she said. They rose from the ground. Martin hooked his jacket over his shoulder and walked slowly around their picnic place.

When she had finished, she called him.

"You're doing it again. Just like the first times. Walking round and round while I clear up. Walking round and round to protect me. It's exactly what you should have done. I do feel perfectly safe with you - and when we are just talking about ourselves, I feel perfectly happy too."

The light had begun to fade. They walked slowly from the spot. Reaching the house, they kissed again and she went inside.

V

Driving home, Martin thought, for a moment or two, about his alibi for the day. It had surprised him how easy it had been to conduct his affair with Liz. It had lasted a long time. The complexities of London, and the varied demands of his work, had made it easy to smuggle into his life the necessary hours. Madge had been undemanding: he had tried to make it up to her. And yet, he would have been shocked to be discovered.

Approaching his home he tried to compose himself, to turn himself into a university teacher returning from an additional, unwanted chore. It had, of course, become easier.

He need not have worried. As he opened the front door, Joan ran up to him, weeping and distraught.

"Mum's been mugged," she said. He saw Edward standing on the stairs, white-faced, afraid to come down.

In the sitting-room Madge sat, silent. A cup of tea stood on the table. Her face was bruised, her eyes closed. Martin put his arm around her shoulders.

"I'll get you something stronger," he said.

Edward now stood at the door. Father was home. One would still have to live through it, but it would be all right.

During the evening John came in. He was shaken, inadequate, no help to them. Later Robert rang: he had already heard.

Madge said little: she seemed to be shocked. She would not talk about it, would not call a doctor, or tell the police. Martin nursed her, bathing her face, turning into a father again. He felt deeply guilty.

All the children were outraged that someone had had the *cheek* to hurt their mother. "We'll never forget it," one said. Only slowly, over days, would they seem to get over it. As her bruises faded they would be comforted, but would see that she was a little different, often silent and preoccupied, sad and damaged.

Next morning neither Martin nor Joan seemed to want to leave her. "You should take a taxi to those classes, Mum," said Joan.

"Not go on the Underground."

"Don't worry, Joan. I might take a rest anyway."

"But you really should be careful, you know."

"I will, Joan."

Martin watched anxiously. "Shall I stay home, Madge?"

"Both of you, don't worry. Alice is coming, anyway. I'll be all right."

They were relieved that they could, more or less, continue with their lives. Slowly they gathered themselves.

"When is Alice coming?" said Martin.

"This morning, Martin. Go on, both of you. Off to work!" She smiled, painfully, and a little wanly.

When Alice came it was her turn to be anxious for her friend. She looked closely into Madge's face, looking for the signs of physical bruising, and of mental consequences.

"I'm so sorry," she said. "I hated it when Jim told me. The way we went on about our boring troubles ..."

"Come in," said Madge. She seemed to hesitate, then went on.

"They weren't boring, Alice. But mine ... it wasn't what everyone thinks."

Alice waited, surprised. They went into the kitchen; Madge filled a kettle.

"I haven't - and won't - tell anyone else. I wasn't 'mugged'. It was a friend ... a man friend."

"Oh Madge! What a foul thing to do."

"He's not foul. As a matter of fact he's very gentle. In many ways he's very like Martin."

"I didn't know - never guessed - that you could have anyone ..."

Alice stopped.

"I'm sorry, Madge. I'm taken aback, I suppose, because you and Martin seem so close ..."

"We are close ... in some ways. I can't explain."

"I shouldn't be looking to see if your bruises have gone, Madge. I should be asking how you are."

"I'm quite bereft, Alice. I feel destroyed, as if everything ... nearly everything, has gone. As though a great hole has been cut in me. Round about here." She passed her hand vaguely around her breast.

Alice took her wrists and held them.

"You could tell me, of course, that I've got Martin, and the children ... it would be like saying: why don't I take cold baths."

"I'm sorry, Madge. I don't think I would have said that."

"It's happened before. Once I was sitting on a beach with the family. No-one knew how I was feeling. I remember looking around and wondering how many of the people I could see had ... a great hole."

"Do you want to talk about it?"

"It helps. I feel better already. I just suddenly thought, when I saw you at the door, why not tell you."

"I'm glad, Madge. Do you want to talk about ... him?"

"Patrick? Not now, Alice. It's all over, anyway. That's what I've got to get used to. If I could talk about that I would. But I don't know how I'll do it."

"I think I understand that."

"Alice ... I'd rather you didn't tell Jim. I know you wouldn't tell anyone else."

"Of course, Madge."

It was, of course, one of the recognised solidarities - one between women.

They settled to their tea ceremony, neither speaking for a time. Then Alice seemed to come to a decision.

"At first, Madge, I'd have thought it disloyal to keep anything from Jim. Now I know I have to."

She seemed to hesitate.

"I haven't told him, for example, about myself. That I'm actually desperate."

"Oh no! Oh Alice. Not you too."

"We keep a reasonably good face on it. Between us as well as outside, as a matter of fact. But I can't stand being in that house, painting my silly abstracts, which don't earn us any money, waiting for the disaster I know is coming. Why ... I don't even paint *bottles*!"

"I'd no idea it was like that, Alice. Of course I have noticed -

we both did - that you two sometimes seemed a bit tense together."

"We could just blow up. I wouldn't blame him - or myself. As a matter of fact, I love him. But I don't know how long I can stand it."

"Stand what, Alice? I mean, what especially?"

"Everything, Madge. Poor Jim. He's not well, of course, and he hates that. We thought it was piles at first. It's a common complaint, the doctor said, with people who are run down, or worried. But it seems he has an anal fissure. It's painful, sometimes crippling. It doesn't help. But what I can't stand is the prospect of *years* ... of trouble ahead. He doesn't quite know how I feel, and he does his best. He has wild schemes of living somewhere else while our house is sorted out - buying a flat, or something. That's when things are going well with his stuff. Then he's euphoric for a time, tries to get commissions with payment in advance. But it would be crazy: it would drive him mad if he got them."

Madge said nothing.

"Madge! I came to see how you were. But I'm telling you how I am."

Now Madge held Alice's wrists. "Go on, Alice."

"And of course, I'm not sure about children. At least I'm ambivalent about them. I think Jim wants them though."

"I wondered."

"And there's another thing, Madge. An old, old story, I'm afraid. I'd rather you didn't mention it to Martin. But the fact is, Jim has a bit of a wandering eye."

"Oh Alice, has he?"

"As far as I know he hasn't actually wandered yet, but I'm very much aware that he might. Why shouldn't he? I'm older than he is, and no beauty."

"Don't be silly, Alice. You're most attractive."

"I know exactly what I am, Madge. Strong, intelligent looking. I think sometimes Jim would like the other thing. The trouble is, I know I mustn't seem to be suspicious. It's insulting, and unattractive. But I can't help it."

"So you see," she went on, "we've got quite a lot to sort out."

"I'm sorry about all this, Alice. And yet, it's cheered me up a little - that I'm not the only one, I suppose."

"Not the only one!"

"I mean, not the only one ... having problems. Of course, I'm a guilty party; you're not."

"As a matter of fact, Madge, if I'd had to guess which of *you* two was more likely to wander, I think I'd have said Martin."

"Really!" Madge seemed to ponder. "I don't think so, Alice. Of course, I can't be sure. I sometimes wondered."

"Don't, Madge. I didn't really think either of you would."

"Of course, practically everyone else seems to. We talk about them. He says there's a sexual 'pecking order' and you can usually tell which of the two will go off."

"You mean the ... higher one goes off?"

Does she mean, Alice thought, that she's higher than Martin? I'm definitely below Jim.

"Madge, let me ask you one thing about ... Patrick. You said he was like Martin. Was he a sort of ... newer Martin? You know, after years of marriage one is supposed to get bored with one's husband, and to want a ... lover. But the lover isn't necessarily better than the husband, just newer."

"Maybe, Alice. That's not how it seems at the time. Yes, of course, he's newer. That's exciting. One doesn't want to go into middle ... old age, without something new, or exciting ... or different."

"What will you do, Madge?"

"I don't know, Alice. There's *got* to be something."

Both were quiet for a time.

"One way or other, Madge, we do seem to be a most unfortunate sex."

They smiled, and Alice went on. "It's cheered me up too."

"Any time, Alice. Do come."

*

Madge had been grateful for the unquestioning sympathy of her family: it had allowed her to conceal the fact that it was not shock, but grief, that they saw.

She could hardly blame Patrick. She had, almost literally, asked to be hit. But, she thought, it must mark the end. He would be ashamed to see her bruises, she ashamed to show them: and the reality which they represented would remain, even when they had faded.

Years before, the affair had begun violently. His marriage was in process of breaking; he lived on his own. She and Martin had known him and his wife: they qualified for each other's parties as both colleagues and friends.

Edward was ill. Each parent, concealing the fact from the other, feared for his life. Doctors could not reassure them because they had not diagnosed his illness; what they could say seemed ominous.

Martin and Madge had found that they could not comfort each other. In suffering separately they had failed to share the most intense experience of their marriage. One night she had walked to Patrick's flat. She was angry with Martin, in danger of abusing him unpardonably, blaming him for their mutual failure. Patrick had seen at once that she was distraught: he set about comforting her. But it was not what she wanted: she wanted to be taken to his bed, and to be used violently. She wanted an experience even more intense. It was her first adultery.

Next morning she knew that they would continue to meet: she presumed that it must be in secret. The excitement of the idea supported her through the rest of Edward's illness. Suddenly he was better; she and Martin shared their joy. But she knew that her life was changed, would now be in two parts.

Cautiously she set up a double life. She pretended an interest in evening classes - in exotic subjects taught at distant institutes: she could not easily be questioned about them. It surprised her that Martin did not seem to want to do so. Then, laying a simple alibi for the afternoon she had, once a week, stayed away for both the afternoon and evening. She was fairly certain that her family did not doubt her weekly alibi. Perhaps they were pleased that she had a small life of her own.

For years the affair had ruled her. She had become one of the freemasonry of deceivers: many of her friends belonged to it but she had not expected to. Patrick had accommodated himself to her routine and at first all had been gaiety and excitement. Only slowly had she begun to despise herself - to despise the phrases, seen in the 'agony columns' of magazines, which described their weekly meetings. They were, indeed, engaged in 'discreet weekly encounters'.

Her self-contempt had grown as the affair became more turbulent. Although he was as deeply involved as she was, she knew that she was in competition with another woman. She knew too that he had temporarily abandoned the other, but not why he had done so. She suspected that the other had not been told even of her existence: it was as though he had wanted to protect for himself the option of returning.

Nursing her bruises, and her grief, she went over and over the thoughts which gave her most pain. It surprised her to find that she was in the habit of standing against a wall, with her back to it, when these thoughts engulfed her. She would stand for minutes, immersed in them, until self-contempt drove her to do something else.

The worst end of an affair was to be plainly rejected. But she knew that the fear of rejection was itself destructive: of itself it drew on the end. As doubts grew between lovers, it might be that each partner would begin to watch for the moment at which he could withdraw safely, *before* he was rejected. At best, there would be a decent, civilised ending by both at the same time. She envied those who could deal thus simply with their lives. But she could not, and because of it, her hurt was greater. She wondered whether, for her, a violent ending was perhaps best.

Was it the case, she wondered, that a love affair must either grow or diminish? And that as soon as it began to diminish, as soon as both recognised that, there was the danger of an end? Was it not a sort of accelerated marriage?

She knew that she had drawn on the end by her own anxiety. She remembered times when she had tried to test the strength of her lover's attachment to her. It was a silly practice, like pulling at a screw in plaster to test its hold. Eventually the act itself helped to destroy the hold: the screw would come out.

In those familiar sentences - 'I don't think you really love me' ... 'perhaps we ought not to see so much of each other' - she had been trying to increase his attachment by threatening to reduce her own. It had only irritated him. Then she had, ostentatiously, refrained from doing so: that too had irritated him. But nothing made any difference to the reality. If there was a reasonable hold, and no-one in competition, it would go on. If there was competition it would depend absolutely on which had the greater hold. Here it was, indeed, a 'pecking order'. But the two of a couple must themselves be fairly close on that register if there was to be the hope of success: if they were not, it was mere amusement for one, and ultimately pain for the other.

What had been irresistible was that he had seen that the explosive start of their affair must be discounted, that she must be respectfully seduced as though it had not happened. He had done it gently.

For the hundredth time she imagined him behind her, playfully - but deliberately - fitting his hands to her waist in the way only he had done. It was absurd how much depended upon the sequence - the progression - of physical acts. Why were they so important? Was it only because they were with a new person: were they the symbols of the new person?

She knew that for years her relationships with her family had been maintained only through habit and good nature, and because of Patrick - only because her centre was elsewhere. Now, presumably, it would be harder. They'll think it's the menopause, she thought.

She must - soon - tell Martin about her affair. She was fairly sure he had not suspected her. But she knew that her motive was not generous: it would be for her own comfort if she did so. She was sure that he would not only understand, but would be pained by her present pain, even though hurt by her betrayal of him. A desire for this warmth - as well as for the dissipation of her guilt - tempted her, but it would not be fair. She was, too, afraid of what he would first say.

VI

Martin, though professor, and ostensibly head of his department, did not feel that he was quite in control of it. It seemed to him that he was in dispute with Booth, his co-professor, and that it was not a dispute about policy, but a trial of strength; that it was undeclared, but known to both.

He had known of departments in which two senior members engaged in continuous struggle, so that their juniors, keeping a wary eye upward, went about their own business without reference to them. He had known of departments in which the head was already a cipher - the tool of one of his junior colleagues, or of his secretary, or even of his own wife, mysteriously implanted into the system. All were the occasions for amused contempt. Academic, common-room gossip was merciless: Martin had engaged in it himself. Now he was in danger of being its butt, playing a part in one of these scenarios. Universities, colleges and their departments were recognised microcosms - arenas in which warriors could practise their craft in relative safety, free from the risk of death, or bankruptcy.

But even to have it seen that such a struggle existed in his own department would have been a humiliation for him. So, while engaging in it, he must pretend that it did not exist, must hide his own involvement in it even from those closest to him: that made it harder. It made it harder too that his enemy was younger. Ultimately, in one way or other, a younger adversary was bound to win.

He could not even relish the engagement: every confrontation, every stand taken, caused his meter to register distress, his adrenalin, blood, or acid - he was not sure which - to churn. He thought that for some of his colleagues that was not the case: that they enjoyed it all; he suspected it to be true of his own Provost. It was an inestimable boon.

"Ah, Martin," said the Provost, "... how nice of you to come."

"Of course, Ted," said Martin. "I heard you wanted to see me."

"There's something I want your advice on, Martin, and I don't really have anyone to ask."

Martin waited: the preamble signified nothing. The matter upon which the Provost wanted advice might not even be the occasion for the interview.

It was not. "And I did want to talk to you, Martin," said the Provost, later, "about *things in general* ..."

For Martin it was a joke phrase. He and a colleague had exchanged a glance of amusement on hearing, in the common room, the head of a department speaking the phrase to one of his juniors - an assistant whose period of probation was nearing its end.

"I've very much admired the way you've handled the Faculty ... as Dean," he went on. "I know it's not easy ... some of them are a little awkward, I dare say. But reports are ... that you have the handling of it ... beautifully. It's especially important just now."

Whose reports, Martin wondered.

"And your research ... outstanding, as we've always known, and at last properly recognised ... brings credit on us all, of course."

"It's kind of you to say so, Ted. The fact is, that particular piece of work came out quite a few years ago."

"Ah, but ... I'm sure there is just as good to come."

Not so, thought Martin.

The Provost stopped for a moment.

"How you do it all ... and run your Department, completely beats me."

He stopped again. Martin knew that he would come, at the correct moment, to the point. Perhaps the approach had been too quick. He took cigarettes and a long holder from a pocket.

"I know you don't, Martin."

He fitted and lit the cigarette, and drew on it.

"Have you ever thought, Martin ... about shedding some of that?"

"You mean, Ted, giving up as Head of Department?"

The Provost said nothing.

"Is that what you do mean, Ted?"

"Well, just give me your reaction ..." The Provost stopped, and waited.

"Well, yes ... I have sometimes thought of it. Not as an immediate proposition, but ... in a few years' time, I think I might be quite glad of it."

"I'm sure you're right, Martin."

"I suppose," said Martin, "as there are only two other professors in the Department, and Bruce could hardly take it on, it would be Tony Booth. Let him have five years'." He had named his putative enemy.

The Provost seemed pleased.

"I've really been very gratified," he said, "that so many heads of departments - appointed, after all, on the old system - have seen the point of *rotation*. Inevitable, I suppose, in present circumstances. It's not a life job for anyone who really cares about the product - as you do, Martin."

It was true, thought Martin, that he cared about the product. He hoped that the Provost meant students. It was true, also, that many of his colleagues now favoured the rotation of headships of departments. But the Provost's undisguised enthusiasm for the untraditional procedure was disingenuous. It was that which ensured his own supremacy. Five years was not quite long enough for a head of department to find where real power lay: at the end of his term the professor would hand over his baton with relief; his successor as head would start again from the beginning.

"He's a brilliant fellow, Booth," said the Provost. "I know you agree."

"Of course I do, Ted. It was my idea that he should be invited."

"I'm grateful, Martin. Of course, I thought then he was a bit young, but that's how things are going. Everyone says he's a high flyer, but - with luck - we'll have him here for his best years."

He stopped. Martin wondered whether the interview was over. It did not seem so.

"I assume," he said, "that you agree with me, Ted ... that Booth is still some distance off ... I mean, that I should stay on as Head for a few years ..."

"Of course. I agree absolutely. Brilliant, no doubt, but immature ... a little rough at the edges ..."

He paused.

"But I'd like you to consider, Martin, a proposition I've been giving some thought to. Just an idea."

The Provost manoeuvred the cigarette in its holder.

"We both agree, I know, that ultimately - but not yet - the headship should rotate ... we both think Booth was a catch, and we must do all we can to ... hang on to him."

He paused again.

"What would you think, Martin, about *joint* headship?"

"You mean, Ted ... Booth and me, joint Heads of Department!"

"How does it strike you?"

"Is it your idea, Ted? I mean, has it been discussed anywhere?"

"My idea entirely, Martin. As I see it, it would seem to solve quite a number of problems."

"Problems?"

"Well, we've talked about your ... idea to step down, eventually, and about the desirability of keeping Booth with us as long as possible."

"That suggests, doesn't it, that you think Booth would want it. Quite a number of high flyers wouldn't be seen dead in a head of department's chair. At least, not until they've landed the one they're aiming for."

"I've no idea, Martin. As I say, it's my idea. Just something to kick around. I thought it would give him time to get used to the job - without ultimate responsibility. You and he get on well together ..."

"Yes, of course we do."

"Eventually, when ... you felt he was ready for it, you could just hand over - and back to your research. You'll have finished your stint as Dean, and I know that's what you want."

Easier said than done, thought Martin.

"Well, what do you think?"

"I've not had time to think, Ted. I can only tell you my immediate reaction."

Martin knew that he must remain bland; his answer must seem to be objective. He knew also that he would not quite succeed - that he never quite succeeded.

"It seems to me, Ted, just off the top of my head, that that would be to get the worst of all worlds."

"How so?"

"Well ... as you know, I'm not a fanatical supporter of the head of department system. As against the chairman system, I mean. But it's what we've got, and at least, in the system, you know where you stand. If you have a strong, good head of department ..."

"Like you, Martin, if I may say so."

"... thanks, Ted. As I say, if you have a strong, good head, fine. Even if you have a bad one, as long as he's strong, it's tolerable. But precisely because everyone knows where he stands. If the head of department makes a decision, at least it's made, for better or worse."

"Quite right, Martin."

"But *joint* heads! It must be a recipe for disaster. Like having a single, weak one."

It was obvious, Martin thought, that the interview was now coming to an end. The Provost would not press the point at once: it was not his way. But if he was determined upon his proposition there would be an interval, in which Martin would be expected to reflect, and it would be brought up again.

"Well, kick it around a bit, will you, Martin? No hurry, of course."

Martin thought he understood: the Provost was, indeed, determined upon it. He might have said: 'if you like, Martin, we'll kick it into the long grass'; or he might have said: 'let's kick for touch then, Martin'. Either would have indicated that he did not mean to press. All the Provost's metaphors were sporting. It was, of course, his sport.

"And thank you so much for coming to see me."

Martin saw that the Provost had not been totally satisfied by his conduct of the interview: it would be prolonged a little. Conducting Martin toward the door he pointed to a small sculpture on a ledge.

"What do you think of it, Martin? I'm told I ought to have something modern in here. I don't know anything about art, of course. Don't even know what I like ..."

"It doesn't do anything for me, Ted." It was not quite true: it seemed to Martin that the sculpture was empty and derivative: he thought he knew the derivation.

A small committee had been charged with the duty of spending a tiny sum each year on the purchase of art works. The results, dispersed feebly about the tall corridors and common rooms, had generated - to the obvious pleasure of the Provost - controversy and bad temper.

"I couldn't agree more, Martin." The Provost sighed. "Of course, we have to have committees. But all that counts around here has been done by individuals. You, for instance. I was saying earlier what a fine head of department you've been - and recently Dean as well, of course. But what I've particularly valued ... has been your *steadiness*. I simply don't know where I'd be without it." They had reached the door: the Provost's eyes were beginning to fade.

I won't think about it yet, Martin thought. To be able to put unpleasant matters aside for a time was a necessary technique: he had been glad to discover it; he used it nearly every day.

*

Martin called at a pub on his way home: it was one which Jim used, and he was there.

"I'm glad to see you, Jim," he said. "As you see, I'm having a premarital drink."

"Who got at you, Martin?"

"My Provost. He's so bloody skilful. If he had to tell me I was redundant he'd made me think it was my idea."

"Is there anything like that afoot, Martin?"

"I have been wondering, Jim, whether that could be what it was all about. He could be sowing a few ideas around, hoping to persuade a few staff that it would be more comfortable out to grass. Just a preliminary round. Save himself trouble later."

"But surely, Martin, you're not old enough for that. You're a head of department, and I thought you had 'tenure'."

"I'll tell you exactly how old I am, Jim. The policemen got younger ages ago. Now I see that people I turned down for jobs are being knighted. And as for 'tenure' ... no-one quite knows nowadays."

"From where I look, Martin, your job seems perfect. But I

expect it's tough, too. I don't think the ... women quite realise it. Someone said that the career struggle - it used to be male - was our equivalent to childbirth, and takes longer. Why do we go in for it? I don't mind admitting, I get pretty frantic sometimes."

"Don't we all, Jim."

"And of course ... home ... doesn't help."

"Home, Jim? You mean your house?"

"It's not just the house, Martin. I find myself coming into the office here," he indicated its direction, "when I ought to be actually *writing* at home. The office is no good for that, and I don't have to be there. But ..."

He hesitated.

"Somehow, just like the play I never wrote, and am not going to write, there really is a ... crack between us. I don't know how bad Alice thinks it is."

Martin listened.

"Of course everything acts on everything else. Poor Alice. She wants children, but can't have any. It looks as though her Fallopian tubes are blocked, and she feels guilty about it. And she feels guilty because she doesn't make much money. But her paintings *are* real. I sometimes think they're the only real things we have."

Jim looked at Martin, went to the counter for more drinks, and spoke again as though he had not stopped. "Then I sometimes think they're just blots. As a matter of fact, Fallopian tubes ... all those female works ... do look like Rorschach blots."

He changed the subject abruptly.

"I've an idea for a play, Martin. Living somewhere in middle-class London, there's a foreign *au pair* girl, doesn't understand English too well, still rather bemused and innocent. Up and down the street, one by one, the husbands and fathers fall for her. We see them making their bids - one over the garden wall, one in the park, one in the pub. They reveal different things - deviousness, naivety, some of them even innocence or nobility. She doesn't quite understand - though we do - and doesn't quite know how serious they are, or how to deal with them. She lays waste to the street, in fact, and doesn't know it. Repercussions in every house, of course. At the end of her time she goes back, to Norway, or Germany, or wherever it is. The children where she lives are sorry, the wives are delighted. The husbands are all a little reduced."

"What will you call it, Jim?"

"I don't know yet."

"What about 'Queen Bee'?"

"That's good. Why not! It's worth a drink. Of course, if I wrote that play, Alice would look around to see if there *was* an *au pair* girl near us. I wouldn't blame her. She doesn't realise - no-one realises - that one doesn't just write about what has happened to one."

He stopped, and seemed to ponder, but then went on.

"Of course, one does tend to write about what's on one's mind. *Au pair* girls, young girls, usually are on my mind."

"Aren't we all the same, Jim?"

"I don't know for sure, Martin. I tell you, sometimes, when I pass a girl in a street, I feel a positive relief when I see that she's not perfect. I'm 'excused', I seem to think. I don't have to do anything about her."

He sighed.

"Unfortunately, so many of them are perfect. It must be all that orange juice, or milk - or was it the orange juice and milk your lot had?"

"I do know what you mean, Jim. But have you noticed ... perfection can come and go? You can be, as you say, 'excused' from doing something about someone, but suddenly you're not excused. Something has taken over."

"What is it, Martin? Is it in her, or in you?"

Now Martin went for more drinks.

"It's funny, Martin, what a few pints can do. I don't really want to tell you about the plays I nearly write ..."

Jim took a large swig of his beer.

"You probably guessed, Martin. Naturally, there's a girl at the office. A *young* girl. Nothing's happened yet, but we've both ... registered."

Martin said nothing.

"I'd be glad, Martin, if you'd not mention that to Madge. I'd rather she didn't know."

"Of course not, Jim."

"Exactly why, I'm not sure. She wouldn't tell Alice, of course. But I wouldn't want her to know I'm even contemplating ..."

"Don't worry about Madge, Jim."

"I don't want her to think badly of me. I like her ... you both, enormously, and Alice does too. But I can't help it ... contemplating, I mean. Those clear eyes ... skin, those curiously moving ways: not art, the real thing."

He seemed tortured. "Men seem to be more tolerant - of each other, anyhow. But really! A girl at the office!"

"I do know about it, Jim. I mean, I know about guilts ... and still going on. I've known for years."

"Really, Martin!"

"I'd be glad if you wouldn't mention it to Alice."

They emptied their glasses, indicating that they would have more, might go on for some time. Perhaps they would ring their wives to say that they would be late.

"I do wish she wouldn't have so many hot baths," said Jim. "She's absolutely obsessive about them."

"But why not, Jim?"

Embarrassment and disloyalty crowded on Jim's face. "Makes her dry, Martin."

VII

When John reached the Swiss chalet he found the village quiet, the roads and fields still covered with snow. He hoped that he would, quite quickly, find the impulse which was to determine one part of his future - the world's opinion - even though he had set aside the rest for the time being. He spent an hour with his books, planning his attack upon them, still determined, but a little appalled at the scale of the task, and at the imminence of his confrontation with it.

In the valley below the chalet stood a hotel. Most of its windows were boarded, but there were lights at one end. It was evening and he went down: he hoped to find a restaurant.

But only toasted cheese and white wine could be served: the skeleton staff were good-humoured, but adamant.

As he climbed back to the chalet he felt elated by the simple beauty of the village, and by the completeness of his solitude. The few people he had seen in the hotel made no difference to it. He began to feel a confidence: he had been right to make the tedious journey, for a purpose which - one might have supposed - could have been achieved by retreating behind the door of his room in the family home. But this was a purer solitude.

Next morning, one or two shops in the village opened for a few hours. His grammatical - but unidiomatic - French allowed him to buy what he needed; he began to enjoy even the practicalities of his solitude - the preparation of his meals, the washing up afterwards. He turned again to his books - the thousands of pages which, at some level, he must reduce into his own understanding. But they had been written for students of systematic habit, whose teachers would have excused them, chapter by chapter, from the necessity to discover the nub of the argument for themselves. He knew the shape of his subject, the sub-divisions, the names, and he had sampled the ideas. Now he must, quickly, discover the argument.

Still appalled at his task, but determined that his attack upon it should be rational - he would not waste time on unessentials, he would not contemplate the possibility of defeat - he completed his approach, and at last began. Day by day, refusing to be diverted, he prised open, one by one, the puzzles which had strewn his path for nearly three years, which he had carelessly allowed to gather. Even if he had been willing to be diverted, there was no possibility of diversion. From his window, looking upward, there was nothing to be seen but snow; looking down, nothing but the snow-covered buildings of the village. His confidence grew, he gathered speed.

About a week after he had arrived in the chalet he was awakened by the sound of bells. He looked through the window: in the valley below were cattle, walking slowly, swinging their cow-bells. He had noticed the snow line moving along the valley; it had at last reached the hotel below him.

The sun was shining; the whole aspect of the valley had changed. The passing of the snow line seemed to signify a quite different world. Almost at once the village, and the hotel, had filled with activity: they were preparing for tourists. He hoped there would not be too many.

He had prepared a programme and found he was, more or less, keeping to it. So each evening, when he was satisfied with the day's work, or tired, he went down to the hotel. He refreshed his body by drinking the house wine, and his mind by writing a diary.

Monday
I can see there is a kind of beauty about mathematics. If I'd taken it seriously all along I might even have enjoyed my course. I would have seen more point to it, at least. But there's no use pretending I could have acted differently.

There's no doubt that I like the pure mathematics better than the applied. It's harder to get my mind around, but more satisfying when I do.

But is it any more than a game? At least, there seem to be as many systems of pure mathematics as anyone likes to invent. And it it's a game, is there a winner? In practice, it seems, it's whoever happens to invent a system that later turns out to be useful. What's so pure about that?

Of course, I'm not even inventing games; I'm only showing I can understand, and reproduce, the games that other people have played, and only if they've become so popular that they've got into the text-books. I'm invited to re-invent little bits of games!

The hotel is cheerful and undemanding. Nice people, though noisy: they seem to be Italian mine-workers - no hope of talking to them. The owners are French, or Swiss. The grandmother is a real personality - very sexy for a grandmother. There doesn't seem to be a grandfather, so I suppose Father is the boss. They don't know anything about me. Perhaps they think I'm a writer.

Tuesday
Am I really a mathematician? Everything that reaches me has been processed, and already guaranteed to have an answer, so I'm not really being tested when I manage to solve something. I don't always succeed, but as I have no tutor here I just have to let it go and do something else. It would be mad to waste time just because I get stuck.

I suppose the point is that this sideways thinking, which I'm practising all the time, is what - if I became very good at it - would show that I was a mathematician after all. Do I want to be?

Part of the pleasure has to do with the symbols. Although I'm only one of millions, there's something pleasing about writing; dx, δx, or Δx, or especially ∂x, and knowing that you belong to the club of people who know exactly what they mean. It's almost sensual to write Σ, or $\int$, and when you take in a new symbol it's really quite exciting. It's not nearly so much fun in pencil, and I'm glad I brought a good pen, and plenty of shiny paper.

Grandma seems to have taken a liking to me. When she isn't taking the money she sometimes talks to me. I understand her perfectly - at least I think so - and my French amuses her but she seems to understand it. I had too much wine the first night but now I know how to space it out. I like it dry, white, and with dew on the little glass jug. At about ten I feel I could stay there - and here - for ever. My determination to keep to my plan must be keeping away the thoughts that might pull me back home.

I don't even think about Josie often. That was a strange episode. I wonder if I really am a writer, and not a mathematician, because I made so much of a little thing.

Wednesday.
The pleasure of *writing* the mathematics could even get in the way. It's the thinking that counts, I suppose. I've noticed people using unnecessary steps in the argument - for my benefit - just because they obviously enjoy the writing of it. I'm still a bit wary of the whole thing. I'm enjoying the fact that I'm keeping to my plan, though, and I'm enjoying the process of keeping to it.

I like the vector symbols, like $\mathbf{r}$. The amount of information they contain is enormous. All the work has been done already, of course, and I'm only using a few authenticated tricks.

The thing about Grandma is that she's so obviously still a woman. She dresses in black, because she's a widow, I expect, but she has brown eyes which look straight at me, and seem to say much more than the words she is actually saying. As a matter of fact, they seem to be saying quite different things. I think she must be about sixty, and her husband died not so long ago. It turns out that she's the boss's mother-in-law, and I can see now that Mother looks like her. There are a few boys who run in and out occasionally.

Thursday
I had a go at Bessel Functions today, and got absolutely stuck. I finally decided that I just don't like them and will leave them out altogether. Weakness? Self-indulgence? I just haven't the time to use up my nervous energy on something I don't like. I don't even know why I don't like them - perhaps they seem a bit arbitrary and only in the text-books because someone knows they come in useful somewhere.

They have a habit of speaking very fast - at their normal speed, I suppose - when not talking to me. I can't follow what they're saying then, and they obviously know I can't, because I know they've sometimes talked about me. They sometimes speed up suddenly when I'm in the conversation and they don't want me to hear something. Mother is a younger (forty) version of Grandma and I like them both. Her face has the same shape, and the same eyes, but she doesn't have the same expression - is it a kind of longing - that Grandma has. She talks to me sometimes. It's fascinating to see them together, though sad to see how little lines, little sags, and little losses of colour, can change one into the other.

They seem to love the hotel, and the work. There's no servility about them, but a sort of pride in keeping the place clean, and the customers happy. Even the Italians seem to try to be nice to me, though I can't understand them, and can hardly reciprocate.

Friday
Got going well today, Bessel Functions safely under the carpet. It would be interesting to try to analyse why I don't like them. Of course there are a lot of other things I couldn't possibly work on, like geography, or chemistry, or nearer home, computing. It just has to be a part of my plan now to use my time on what I quite like - or at least can tolerate - and therefore comes easily.

About Grandma, I realise that Robert would sum her up in a moment, with some vulgar phrase. He'd probably say that he'd put her out of her misery, being God's gift to women. He might, too!

If I do think of her in that way, I see that she'd be no easier for me to approach than any of the others. Her eyes show that she's a full woman still. She must have been beautiful!

So is Mother, but she doesn't have to show it, I suppose, because of Father. There's a bit of fooling about with the Italians, but I think the proprieties are pretty stern and it's all talk. Oddly enough, it's quite indiscriminate, and directed at Grandma as much as Mother. Somehow that seems right and not just courtesy. I wish I could understand better what they all say. Although I know it's all just a game, it would be nice to understand. The Italians sometimes get a bit drunk, and start to sing, but fortunately not too early in the evening.

Even allowing for the fact that Mother has Father, she doesn't project quite the same womanliness as Grandma. I wouldn't have expected to notice a grandmother: it's probably because I'm there every night, and doing not much else except drink wine.

The boss noticed that I'm drinking more slowly than at the beginning, and has started serving me smaller jugs, so that I can have it better chilled. I couldn't understand at first what they were all saying in a long and apparently - but obviously not really - heated discussion, but that's what it turned out to be. How beautifully they speak French. It's shaming to have to expose the dreadful, fifth-form stuff I produce.

There seems to be a daughter as well, just back from school, or college, but I didn't see her, only heard people talk about her, then sounds of an arrival. The family do have an inner home; they don't conduct all their affairs in the open, though one would have thought so at first.

Saturday
She is the most beautiful girl I have ever seen.

Sunday
I took the day off and walked in the valley, as far as the snow line. Although I saw her for only a few minutes yesterday, I've thought about her all day. She was wearing the local traditional dress, and I thought about open-air things, like picnics with wine. I had wine, olives and cheese, and I couldn't bear it that she wasn't there. Of course I haven't said a word to her, or she to me, and I couldn't have asked her to come with me, so again I'm wallowing in fantasy. I couldn't have got within a mile of it. Who am I, anyway? A really rather uninteresting foreigner, a regular customer, but not on easy terms with the other customers. I can't even speak the language!

Curious how the traditional dress, all innocence, braid and flowers, carries a message. They knew what they were doing!

This evening she hasn't been in the café at all. I've waited longer than usual. But she's obviously still about. Of course I can't ask anyone. I've still only seen her once.

Monday
This evening she's back, and on duty in the café, serving wine. She's wearing trousers, and moves in and out between the tables.

Robert would say: 'I didn't know you were a bum man'. Odd how I resent his vulgar clichés. I suppose his purpose *is* to make things vulgar. Why does he do it? Probably because he knows I resent it.

I have never seen anything so strangely beautiful as her body, in trousers, between waist and thigh. Everything she does - if she's standing still, or moving about, or sitting on her stool - it's all exquisitely perfect. I can't stop looking at her.

It's different from the image in the traditional dress - explicit rather than implicit, I suppose - but equal to it because of the perfection. Her body is slightly full, so there are real curves, but they are perfect. What do I mean? What have I got in my subconscious mind that they call on?

The Italians treat her just as they do her mother and grandmother. That pleases me: I would be annoyed if anyone tried to chase her. Of course I don't know where she was on Sunday.

All I've said to her so far is that I want more wine, please miss, in my correct but execrable French. I'm a little afraid that she'll see I'm 'mooning' after her. Although it's flattering, I know it doesn't really appeal to girls. They want men to pursue them in a forthright manner - either humorously, or seriously, but not hopelessly. I know that's where I go wrong.

Tuesday

Tonight the three women are in the café: they all have the same profile. I wish I could draw what I see - the difference between Grandma and Mother, and between Mother and her. And yet, they must, in a way, be all the same. I'm sure, anyhow, that Grandma is as much a woman as Mother. What about her? Perhaps the truth is that with her the appeal is through the body, with Grandma through the eyes - which must be the memory of the body - and with Mother in between.

Of course I've looked at Grandma and Mother to see what happened to *their* waists and thighs: it's only too obvious. Mother has become much fuller, and Grandma, after becoming fuller, I suppose, has become thin and straight. In both of them the simple beauty that calls to that unknown level in my subconscious mind has gone. But somehow - because of her - they do call to me: some sympathy does go out to them. Perhaps that is why artists use old models, or even more strangely, middle-aged or rather shapeless models. Of course, if I could draw, I'd be allowed to 'moon' after her.

Wednesday
Even in my fantasy what do I really want? I think of nothing else, but I still can't answer that question. I don't know anything about her: she has a sweet voice, and always seems good-tempered - in the curiously vigorous way of foreigners - but I don't know what she's really like. Do I not even care that she might be stupid, or mean, or shallow? I have the absurd idea that because she looks as she does, she can't be any of these. But the only answer I can think of to my question is that I'd want her to be exactly as she is, and for me to win her miraculously. What then?

She didn't know that they'd started to serve me wine in small jugs, and I tried to explain. I don't think I really cared, but it seemed an advance over simply asking for more wine. Grandma had to come in, with her high-speed French, to help me. So the only conversation I've had with her - with a verb in it - has been about the size of a wine jug. How indescribably petty! How distant - how opposite - from what I want to say!

I think I could say it in English. I would try it, at least: I know what it is. But to say it in the café, with the noisy, teasing Italians, and my awful French - which she doesn't understand too well ...

Not too many days left: it's absurd even to imagine that I shall achieve anything. Am I only a fantasist? Do I choose fantasies that I know cannot become reality.

Thursday
I must make some kind of approach. All I could do now would be to declare my hopeless love - which she probably wouldn't understand, and wouldn't care about anyway. But I now owe it to myself to tell her. It might just enter her consciousness.

Reading what I've written, I see that I haven't said anything about her face, or her skin, or hair, or anything else. It's because there's no need to. I insist on believing that beauty is indivisible. You can tell by looking at one part whether or not a girl is beautiful: it's so deeply contained, even in the child - and nothing can change it.

But you still have to look at every part: each offers you a revelation, first in its own right, but also in relationship with all the rest.

Take her hands, as she brings my tray and puts it on the table. How subtle and delicate they are, both in shape, and in their movements. But so is the colour of the skin of her face, just to the left and right of her eyes.

Today I thought that as she can't spend all her time in the hotel I would try to catch her out shopping. So I spent some of the afternoon walking about the village. No luck, of course. I should have realised before that it's my only hope of catching her on her own.

It's quite bustling now, with more and more guest houses opening up. The tourists are beginning to take over, well-heeled and well-equipped, with their expensive wives and girlfriends.

The usual evening in the hotel café - a bit fuller because of tourists. So she's busier than before. I've watched her again, trying not to show it. My presence in the café has dwindled to nothing: I am just one of the tourists who happened to come earlier than the rest. Of course I hate them and wish I could disown them dramatically. What's more likely is that I'll get dragged into some boring, tourist conversation about what sort of day I've had. They are only in the café to pass the time; I am there to see, and watch, a beautiful girl. I suppose she must be about eighteen, or seventeen.

Friday

This afternoon I went into the village again. I thought I'd buy something ridiculous for Mother, some drink for Father, and perhaps something for Joan; but really I only wanted to catch her on her own.

This time she was there, but with her mother. They were obviously shopping from a list, and when I passed they smiled at me, and I smiled at them. I tried to keep them in sight without showing myself. I suppose I had some mad idea - like asking them to join me in a cup of tea! Somehow, seeing her outside the hotel, being recognised as a person, and not just as a customer, is important for my fantasy, but of course nothing came of it. I might have guessed she'd be with her mother.

How strange that it was the perfection of her body between waist and thigh that captured me, and that it was my eye that recognised it. Even if I understood what the ideal was that my eye was referring to - and of course I don't - it amazes me how accurate the reference is. I must be identifying shapes, distances and sizes to an accuracy within millimetres, at a distance from me of metres, as either conforming, or not conforming, to that unknown ideal. Not only as a shape: when it is moving that has to conform, or not, to an ideal of a body in motion. That means that I'm actually comparing *velocities*!

I have some idea how the brain could cope with the job of making such exact comparisons. At least, it's big enough. Don't frogs actually *see* velocities? As the one whose brain is doing it I'm still stupefied. Why does it do it? And what is that ideal?

Exactly at the centre is the point, the apex, the focus, which every male seeks, and finally finds. Oddly enough, that doesn't seem to play a part in what my eye sees, and what my brain does with it. I expect Robert wouldn't agree. He has a simple philosophy about it all.

Saturday

If nothing else, I shall take away, as a memory of these weeks, an indescribable softness. This afternoon I walked in the village again, but she wasn't there. This evening, in the café, she's wearing traditional dress again. But she's with friends, and not on duty, so she's even further away from me. Hard to say whether any one of them is a boyfriend, but there are several bronzed, knickerbockered youths who look like mountain guides.

That might have been all. But I collided with her in the corridor. She was coming from the lavatory, I was going to it: it could hardly have been a less romantic place for an encounter. As we collided, I felt her indescribable softness, my hand pressing into it. It was all so obviously an accident that she was not even embarrassed, only apologetic, for her clumsiness, I suppose. I apologised for mine.

Sunday

I've heard the 'bus every morning, hooting as it makes the great turns up the mountain. I never thought she would have gone back so soon - wherever she goes. Tonight she wasn't in the café. Grandma was there, and in my pathetic French I asked where her grand-daughter was. She had already gone, she said, on the 'bus this morning. She answered in the nice French way, full of adjectives and politeness, and with those eyes still saying something more - or even different.

The Italians have gone now and it's all tourists. *She* has gone. I must try to keep her - and that softness - out of my mind. I think it'll be a long time before I forget her.

*

Robert and Connie were at a party: their hosts, and most of the guests, were her friends from another era - young executives, clerks, typists - and their friends. It was not a party of the young and irresponsible, nor of Bohemians: these were turning toward ambition. But they needed parties where they could resume irresponsibility for a time, where they could, perhaps, leave something to chance. The misdemeanours of teenage parties were not acceptable; sexual boldness and controlled drunkenness were. The guests had arrived in pairs; the same pairs were likely to leave together.

Connie seemed pleased that she could display Robert as her capture. "Where did you get him?" one girl said. The questing eyes of other girls said the same. There was loud music; the guests danced in one area, and retreated from it as far as they could if they wanted to talk. Half-drunk glasses of wine and beer lay on all horizontal surfaces. Progressively the guests had abandoned their ownership of glasses and now took whatever was to hand. The hosts circulated, plying them with drink.

As soon as he and Connie were separated, Robert felt uneasy: he had felt the same before. He knew that it was the explicit sexuality of the girls that disturbed him. Even though they were, ostensibly, neutralised by their partners, there was too much left over: it hung in the air.

He had thought he could handle Connie. At least, he had succeeded so far. But the concentrated, determined, massed sexual charge in the room dismayed him. He felt inadequate: he had strayed into the wrong league. But it did not seem to be an orgy. He looked around for Connie.

"So you're Connie's," said a girl to him. "I'm Sharon."
"Hello, Sharon," he said. "And whose are you?"
"Oh ..." she indicated, absently, someone behind her.
"Dance?"
"If you like."

They wormed their way into the moving part of the crowd. Loosely coupled, but not touching, they wriggled in the accepted manner. She looked steadily at him: he was not sure whether her expression denoted admiration or contempt: it was a sophisticated, contemporary face. Her movements were explicit, unequivocal. That, of course, was the style of the dance. But she had transcended it: she emitted an uncompromising, thrusting sexuality.

"Come on," she said. "Let's sit." She picked up a glass. He followed her, and they sat on the stairs. She sat above him, showing her long legs.

"Tell me about yourself," he said.

He knew it was foolish: she had already done so.

She did not speak; her expression, he now saw, denoted contempt.

"Let me get you some more wine." She said nothing.

He fought his way to the drinks. Connie had become one of the dancers, and waved cheerfully.

Sharon had not moved; he gave her the wine. She looked directly, arrogantly, into his eyes.

"You're a *poof*," she said.

Bored, she climbed down the stairs and joined the crowd. Absently, without a partner, she gyrated among the other dancers.

He left the party and went into the road. It was raining. Buses, precariously balanced on their skidding wheels, passed every few seconds. I would only have to step into the road, he thought. They wouldn't be able to stop.

He was overwhelmed by the insult. He had been overwhelmed by accusations before, and he knew that it had been when they were true. He stood on the edge of the pavement, annoying and alarming the 'bus drivers.

But, he thought, I'm not attracted to men. He went back into the party, now wet and bedraggled. He sat on the stairs and looked around the room.

What about him, he thought. A young man had turned to look at him, and held his gaze for seconds. But I'm revolted, thought Robert. Revolted, not attracted.

"Whatever happened to you?" said Connie.

"Too much drink," he said. "Had to breathe some air."

"Poor old thing!" She sat with him on the stairs, linking her accredited arm with his.

The young man had turned away. Robert wondered at the strength of his revulsion, uncertain of it.

VIII

Martin was on his way to lunch with the Provost; he did not know who the other guests were to be. The Provost's private lunches were notorious. "If you want to know what is going to happen," one of Martin's colleagues had said, "and not what the Academic Board, or the Senate, or Council, think is going to happen, or think they have decided is going to happen, just find out who is lunching with the Provost."

He was not in the mood for it. He wanted neither to join a campaign, nor to defend his position against campaigners. He felt ill, so ill that he thought of staying away, but did not.

"Ah, Martin," said the Provost, "of course you know Sir John ... and Sir Robert." A beadle approached with a tray of drinks.

Sir John was the head of the department from which Tony Booth had come, and a powerful name in the field. He was, in the ironic jargon, Tony's 'Great White Father'. Martin thought he understood: the Provost's purpose was to persuade him, by flattery, to give up the headship of the Department. The smallness of the party was, in itself, flattering. Martin wondered whether he would discover why the Provost, and presumably Sir John, were so anxious to bring it about.

Sir Robert would be an onlooker in the argument. He was a banker, a lay member of the Council, surely invited to add weight, and to be flattered in his turn. At Council he would know of the matter, so his support could be counted on. Lay members did not always get things right, but they knew how to act. In his own time on Council Martin had heard some of their principles expressed: they were simple and strong. 'Feller's innocent till he's proved guilty'. 'Back the man at the helm'.

In the presence of the larger than life, Martin had always found himself a little louder, a little larger than life, and some shades away from reality. He could not help it, although he despised it. He respected Sir John as a scientist, but disliked him as a political figure; with Sir Robert he would have nothing in common. But he must inflate himself a little: he was unwilling to seem to be in the wrong company; it was even discourteous.

"The trouble with governments," said Sir Robert, at lunch, "is that they never have to balance their books. Don't you agree, Ted?"

Listening to the Provost, and even to Sir John, Martin realised that they, too, were inflating themselves slightly. Only Sir Robert was acting normally.

Martin felt again the new pain in his chest.

"What do you think, Blake?" Sir Robert's was a booming voice, accustomed to booming, and to being answered quietly.

Martin prepared to answer him, quietly and seriously. But he knew he was ill: he wished that he could, again, find moist grass to lie on; he wondered whether he could lie on the carpet.

"Are you all *right*, Blake?" said Sir Robert: he seemed angry.

Martin found that the Provost was holding his shoulders.

"Damned near fell into your soup, Blake!" said Sir Robert. "If Ted hadn't caught you."

He mounted his strength.

"I'm sorry, Ted ... gentlemen ... sorry to ruin ..."

"Come on, Martin," said the Provost. "Let me take you in there. Just have a rest."

"I'm very sorry, Ted ..."

"Don't upset yourself, old chap. Happens to us all."

Martin rose carefully and walked slowly into the Provost's office. The pain had gone, but he knew that his clothes were again sodden with sweat.

"Just sit there, Martin. We'll go ahead."

He was relieved. As it had become inevitable, he was glad to be recognised as ill. The booming and the laughter in the next room showed that he had not upset his fellow guests. He could not hear what was being said, but it did not seem that they could be seriously considering any matter. No doubt the Provost thought there was no need to hurry. It was not reassuring: it might be that the projected move was to be only the first in a much larger sequence. The Provost always took a very long view.

In precarious times not only staff, but departments and institutions could become redundant. Those in the know, or fortunately placed, or sufficiently buccaneering, emerged with larger empires. Their less fortunate colleagues went to grass.

When younger, Martin would have drawn his own battle lines. Now he began to feel that he was a piece in another's game. Let it go, he thought. I wonder if this moment is my turning point. Downhill from now on, perhaps.

The Provost came to the door.

"That's more like it, Martin."

Martin settled to rest, and to recover. He resented, slightly, the Provost's obvious good health.

The Provost came back. "I've asked old Twigg to have a look at you," he said. "Before we send you home. He'll be along in a minute or two. Physician of the old school, of course. Looks at your toes if you tell him you've got a sore throat. However, he's usually right."

Twigg was cheerful and workmanlike; he looked at Martin for a few minutes.

"Do you belong to any of these private health schemes?"

"Yes, I do, as a matter of fact." Martin was, of course, ashamed of it.

"Well," said Twigg, "if I were you I'd go along to this feller ..." - he wrote a name and address - "... privately, and get him to check you over. I'll have a word with him. Through your doctor, of course. Don't leave it too long. And take it easy for a week or two."

"All right, Martin?" said the Provost, as cheerfully as before. "I'll order a taxi for you."

"I have got my car, Ted." The Provost looked at Twigg.

"What do you think, Harry?"

"Oh yes, I think if he waits a bit longer ... Just wait until you feel normal ... and go carefully. And let me know how you get on."

Returning to his office, Martin found one of his technicians waiting.

"Sorry, Prof," he said. "Your secretary told me you would be back. Can I have a talk with you?"

Martin hesitated.

"Just come in for a minute, Mr Sexton," he said. "I may have to put you off, but just tell me what it's about."

They sat in the office. Sexton seemed to be under stress. Martin had not spoken to him for some time.

"How *are* you?" he said. "We haven't talked recently."

"I've not been up to much ... down here." He touched his stomach. "A bit of that again ..."

"I'm sorry to hear it," said Martin. "I had noticed you didn't look quite ..."

"I'm under medication, of course. Taking the tablets I had before."

He stopped.

"Can I speak bluntly, Prof?"

"Of course you can: you know that. I might have to stop you and say I want someone else's opinion as well, but ... go ahead."

"Well, Prof, did you, or did you not, put me in charge of the modelling shop?"

"Yes, I did, Mr Sexton. I'm quite clear about that."

"And did you, or did you not, put Mr Sweet in charge of the repair shop?"

"Yes, that's quite right, I did. I suppose ... you're going to tell me it isn't working out."

"I know you mean well, Prof, and I'm sorry I've had to come to you again."

Martin saw that Sexton was ashamed - that he had not been able to handle whatever worried him.

"The fact is, Prof, Mr Sweet is moving in on me ..."

"Are you sure about that? I know how easy it is for misunderstandings to arise ..."

Martin felt tired, and anxious about driving home.

"No doubt about it. And I'm not the only one who's noticed. I could mention a few names. He's even boasting about it."

"But surely ... what I arranged is absolutely clear!"

"That's just it, Prof. It isn't. He's bound to use my shop, and I'm bound to use his ..."

"But Mr Sexton, that's why I laid it down ... who was in *charge* in each shop."

He stopped.

"I see ... that it can't be quite as simple as I thought. But I'll have to see you again, I'm afraid. I really have to go."

Martin saw, on Sexton's face, in about equal measure, the expressions of hope and distrust. He knew that Sexton's class had a generalised distrust of its masters. Confidence grew when nurtured from above: he thought he had succeeded in nurturing it with most of his technicians. What, thought Martin, will he tell his wife when he gets home? Would he say: 'he doesn't give a damn', or 'he won't do anything about it'? Or perhaps he would say: 'I told Prof. He's going to look into it', and keep his doubts to himself. That was more likely.

"I won't drop it, Mr Sexton," said Martin. "Just come into my secretary's office and we'll fix a time to talk about it."

It was Friday afternoon. Departmental troubles usually seemed to reach him then. It was as though the protagonists had hesitated throughout the week to bring them into the open, but had decided at last that they could not survive the weekend without having done so. The solutions, inevitably, must wait for a new week.

This one did not seem to Martin to be too serious. He was fairly sure that Sweet was the buccaneer and Sexton the victim. It simmered constantly: its very visibility meant that it could be controlled.

What he feared, what sometimes hovered over his weekends were the sudden manifestations of worse dangers. They rarely came from academic staff, protected as they seemed to be by standing in the larger world. But the affairs of technicians, secretaries, students especially, sometimes erupted unexpectedly and dangerously. There had been suicides in other departments, none yet in his.

At home, Madge and Joan were surprised to see him.

"You're not feeling well, are you, Dad," said Joan, at once anxious, and severe again.

"Afraid not, Joan. Practically fainted into the soup, as a matter of fact. Lunching with the Provost. Three 'Sirs' in all. Ruined it as a social occasion, I should think."

Both looked severe: he was being too flippant.

"Will you go to bed?" said Madge.

"No, I don't think so. I'll have a bath ..."

"Leave the door open, Dad. I'll bring you a hot drink afterwards. And see a doctor. Promise?"

"Yes, Joan, I will. As a matter of fact, it's fixed up."

"Do you think I ought to go, Mum?" said Joan, when Martin had gone upstairs. "Dad doesn't look too good, does he."

"Of course you must go, Joan: It's your holiday. Don't worry about it. I'll keep an eye on Dad, and I don't mind being at home at all. Nobody need worry."

Joan and Brenda belonged to a sailing club; for years they had spent holiday weeks with their contemporaries, sailing on the Broads. It had begun when family holidays had seemed to become more and more absurd and irrelevant. For both sides - parents and their adolescent children - the sailing club brought freedom and relief. Parents felt assured that their children would enjoy themselves, that it would improve their health and social ease - the members managed the club themselves - and they hoped there would be safety in numbers. The children, released at last, could live in their own way and enjoy any pleasures open to them. It was a fair contract. Neither side talked too much about it: there was no point in rocking the boat.

But this holiday would be, for Joan, a clandestine operation. She and Bryan would be on their own, not with the club. Brenda would, where necessary, provide the alibi.

"Thanks, Mum. Are your sure?" She was enormously relieved.

*

Martin, expensively X-rayed by one specialist, now sat in another's waiting room.

"It's all a matter of plumbing," the first had said. "Very superior plumbing, of course, and self-repairing to some extent. But sometimes we have to ... interfere with it a bit."

The waiting room was shared by several specialists. The patients sat, each with his own, personal, plumbing defect - a constriction, a blockage, a leak, a case of spreading rust. Each had been able to carry it to his appointment, and would carry it home afterwards. For some the defect would turn out to be repairable, for others not: for them it was a time-bomb. For money, a specialist would say whether one was likely to live.

"Ah, so it was old Twigg who put you on to me," said the specialist. He was obviously delighted to talk about his old friend: his reminiscences went back a long time.

"I'm told it's all a matter of plumbing," said Martin later, "and that what I've got is a leak. I used to know all about them."

"So I understand," said the specialist. "But I thought biology was all X-rays and molecular models these days. Where do the leaks come in?"

"It's a bit of everything. My department happens to be large: it grew in the ... expansive days. We even have stuffed animals! My own work, when I got to it, was to do with very pure preparations - hence the leaks."

"I suppose like me, Professor Blake, you're in the age group which thinks it's been caught across a complete change in the nature of his subject. We can't quite join the new, but don't want to be stuck with the old."

Martin felt an urge to talk about himself, to take full advantage of his position. It seemed that as a private patient he was entitled to do so, was allowed extra time for it.

"I know what you mean," he said. "But I've come to the conclusion that it happens to every scientific generation, not only ours."

"As to leaks, I must say I've had quite a few," he went on. "When I was a research student, and even after that, any experiment could be ruined by a leak. A lot of them were: careers were ruined by leaks. One developed a skill about them - I think I was lucky. Fate was kind and allowed me a few crucial leak-free experiments. Then, when I was a lecturer, just beginning, buying a house beyond my means of course, the roof leaked. Could have been disastrous, but it just survived - with patching. But I couldn't afford the time to rebuild my experiments, and I couldn't afford a new roof. And now ... it seems I've got another leak."

"Well," said the specialist, "in a sense surgery is a patching job, but often extremely successful - better than the original sometimes. Unfortunately, we can't replace the whole roof!"

"Yes ... but we often found that the repair caused something else to go wrong nearby ..."

The specialist smiled. "True. It's part of my job to assess the chance of that happening."

The preamble was over. "Just slip off your shirt, will you, Professor Blake, and lie on the couch. I'll prod you around a bit, and then we'll have a few tests."

The door opened a little. "Thank you, nurse," said the specialist. A clean urine bottle had been placed on a shelf. The room seemed to contain very little apparatus, but the specialist's desk was large and impressive.

At last he finished. "Just get dressed, and we'll have a talk."

He waited.

"It might not come to surgery ... I don't know what you feel about that ... or it might, eventually, be a matter of choice. Naturally, one doesn't recommend it lightly."

"Choice? You mean, between having an operation ... and just keeping going?"

"That's right. You'll have to take things easily ... and there'll be medication, of course. It might hold it. But you could have more attacks, and they could get worse. Then, I think, I'd have surgery. Get to the cause!"

Surely, not exactly the *cause*, thought Martin. I think I know the cause.

"Can you ... is it possible to say what the chance of success would be if I had the operation? I mean, is it three out of four, or nine out of ten ... or ten out of ten? If it's ten out of ten, why not have it, and get it over?"

The specialist hesitated.

"It's very hard to answer that. I suppose I could give a figure if I looked up the records of people who've had it, but every case is different, and some obviously have, from the beginning, a better chance than others."

"Is mine ... a more serious case, then?"

"Middle to serious, perhaps. Let me put it this way. My advice is, just take it easily for a time. You know, take some trouble about it; set time aside for it. I don't imagine you do at present. You'll have to have tablets, of course. Come and see me if you have more attacks ... and in three months if you don't. If we decide on surgery, the man I'd like to see do it - he'd have to see you first, of course - really is top man in this line. You do belong to a private health scheme, don't you?"

Martin nodded.

"You'd have to convalesce, of course ... two or three months - the longer the better. You might be able to choose the time to suit you."

So, thought Martin, as they passed through the waiting room, it's a sort of leak. It'll still be there, but we're reducing the pressure. It would, of course, have ruined an experiment, because the results would have been wrong.

"Tell me, Professor Blake, how are students behaving these days? Do you have any trouble?"

"Not to speak of. I think it's because in my subject we still know more than they do."

Driving home, Martin thought about some of the uncompleted tasks which he might have to put aside. It did not seem to him that any disastrous consequence would follow. If they're so unimportant, he thought, why do they fill my time? Why do I tie myself up with it all? Is it just men's games? He remembered days of pleasure when, as a boy, he had sometimes been ill, with a proper, named illness, and had been allowed to stay at home, or even in bed. He would be in the same position again - perfectly entitled to leave homework untouched.

He was disappointed to find that Madge was not at home. Of course, he thought, it's Thursday. He remembered Sexton. I must sort that one out, he thought. He took a card from his pocket and wrote: 'Sexton'. There were other notes on the card. Seeing them, he realised that his system was not working. It was no use making notes if one never looked at them.

But he knew that his mind, just below consciousness, was full of them. With luck the right one would come to the surface at the right time. It was remarkable how often it happened: it was the only system he had been able to use.

IX

Madge soon found her Thursdays, when she might have seen Patrick, too hard to be borne. One Thursday she walked to Victoria Station and took the train to Brighton. Walking on the promenade, or leaning on its railing, she used her sudden freedom in the only way she could: here she could suffer the grief of her broken affair without the effort of concealing it. She worked through the familiar sequence of thoughts, testing herself.

She walked through the narrow streets, looking at the small shops. She loved the shops which seemed to sell one thing only - perhaps coffee, or coloured paper, or cork. Perhaps she would set up a shop of her own! She loved, too, the antique shops, but did not know what she wanted to find there.

In a house agent's window a small, terraced house was advertised and she went to see it: it excited her. Walking on the promenade again, an hour before she must catch her train, she planned a lifeline. If she bought the house she could, occasionally, be secret as well as alone. Brighton was anonymous: one need not be in relationship with it because anyone could go there. She was practised in the female art of invisibility, in indicating that she meant to be alone.

She had helped her mother buy a small house. Next morning she saw the solicitor they had used. She had money because of a legacy, in which Martin had insisted he was disinterested. "I want you to be as easy about money as I am," he had said. She was not sure that he was, even now, always easy. But she was grateful for it. She had always been grateful for his detachment in such matters: she was sure it was courtesy, not indifference.

Over the weeks she bought the house, working through the familiar complexities of that operation. As soon as the vacation was over she began to visit it every Thursday. She bought furniture in the small second-hand shops, and cleaned and decorated the house austerely. Eventually she began to live in it, briefly: it was always there, with its refrigerator cold, its water-heaters ready, and one or two letters from the official world waiting.

She cooked meals for herself, lay in hot baths, read newspapers in her armchair. She imagined that she might, later, increase her occupation: eventually, she might even have Brighton friends. It pleased her that the train from London to Brighton took one hour exactly, and that she lived in London within walking distance of Victoria Station.

Instinctively, she kept her two lives quite separate: the newspaper she read in her Brighton home was not the one to which she and Martin subscribed; she never carried food to Brighton, or to London. Among her neighbours were artisan families of the town, and young commuters to London. They were so different from each other that the oddness of her own occupation of the house need cause no comment: nothing was expected of her. As the reality of her second home grew, she began to attend to its tiny garden, looking ahead to the summer. She was not quite sure what was her purpose, but she had a lifeline, a small existence. She found that she could be, occasionally, not only alone, and secret, but free.

It surprised her how easy it had been to establish a second identity. No-one in London or Brighton knew of her identity in the other place. At times she was not quite sure which of the two was real. She supposed that if she had decided to disappear altogether from London it would have taken the official world - the world of electoral registers, national insurance, income tax - a long time to find her. Even that gave her independence. It suited her mood: she had not wanted to look into the future. Though not happy, she was at least engaged. The family were pleased with what they saw.

Leaving the house, Madge checked carefully the doors and switches. In the London train it occurred to her that nearly everyone - perhaps even Martin at some time - must have been through an ordeal like hers. It was slightly reassuring. She wondered whether she was beginning to come out of it.

Perhaps, later, she and Martin would use the house together. It had been with Martin that she had explored Sussex; they had toyed with it, pretending that they might move to Brighton. She imagined, ruefully, the pleasant but unexciting times they might spend together, and rejected the thought. It was not what she wanted. For the present it must be hers only.

Perhaps later he would be amused to discover her secret; her children, too, would recognise its innocence. They were an understanding family, when they knew what was to be understood.

As the train approached London she sat in the buffet car with a drink. Her thoughts moved back to the ordinary. She would have to go out early next day to do the weekend shopping and she must decide what they would have for lunch on Sunday.

*

Sitting in his college office, Martin was surprised, and annoyed, to hear that his mother was outside, asking to see him.

"Hello, Mother! What a nice surprise."

"I just thought I'd come up to town, just for a day out ..." She adopted an expression, long familiar to him - a simulated wickedness. It suggested that she did not often do that sort of thing.

"And I thought, as I'm here, I'll just see how Martin is. Of course, if you're busy, I won't stay ..."

He knew that she relished his importance, enjoyed being led past secretaries.

She described the difficulties of her journey.

"Did you tell Madge you were coming? I'm sure she'd love to see you."

"No, I haven't, Martin. I don't want to ..."

"Oh, go on, do, Mother," he said quickly. He did not want to hear the word, whatever it might be.

"Well, perhaps I'll ring her." He knew she would not.

"I can't stay. I just wanted to know how you are. I asked for Professor Blake, of course. They didn't seem to know who I meant. Of course he's *Professor* Blake, I said. So they looked down the list again, and found it, of course."

Martin settled into the condition of wary inattention in which he listened to his mother. He must answer direct questions, and listen for them, but he need not otherwise contribute. Joan had often noticed it: severely she had flashed her silent signals, telling him to pay more attention to his mother.

She had begun to speak about one of her neighbours. "I was telling her, *all* my children have made successes of their lives. It made Father very proud of them when he was alive, and he would have been very proud today."

He remembered the tall, stooped figure of his father, grey with despair at one more sign that his children proposed to set up their own lives, that they had rejected his patterns for them.

"They never gave us a moment's trouble; they all married fine people, and now they have fine children of their own. And I told her, it's no accident. It starts in the home, I said. It's no accident that I'm welcome at their homes. I told her that your brother, and Edna, asked me if I would stay with them for ... a few weeks. Of course, I said I'd love to, if they were quite sure ..."

"Of course they are, Mother. I'm sure they'd love to have you. And you know the children do."

"Did I tell you about Mark? Apparently he's doing very well: he's at head office now. And Julie, she's school captain, of course ..."

She went through the register of his five nephews and nieces. I wonder what she says about my kids, he thought. She hasn't much to go on, actually.

"And David has a girlfriend, you know. Apparently it's quite serious." She had put on the manner which he hated, the amused condescension, which she used when skirting around that subject.

"Really!"

"Of course, I don't know if they're *engaged* yet."

"But how are *you*, Mother?" A look of resignation came into her eyes as she began to tell him.

His attention wandered again. Wary inattention was the best response any of them, as adults, had been able to offer their parents. Neither agreement nor participation was possible; fortunately, argument was now unnecessary. On that pragmatic basis they had continued the operation of the family, visiting the old home at the right times, taking the children there to set up that relationship for them. Martin's children had been tolerant, and generous.

But after his father's death his mother had become a problem - to be shared as fairly as could be agreed. It was her professed determination not to be a problem that was the problem. No-one knew what she really wanted, so they had set up fictions. In exasperation, one had said: "why shouldn't even a stupid woman have her desires satisfied - or at least, what she imagines, or pretends, are her desires?" She had no understanding of what was going on around her. Often hurt, sometimes dismayed, she floundered from one awkward posture to another.

"So I told her, when Father was alive, we never felt the need for television, black-and-white, or colour ... we happened to enjoy ... conversation, reading ... and making our own entertainment ..."

The books had remained on the shelves, unopened, and the piano had remained, unplayed, and untuned. "It has a very good tone" she had once said angrily in a family argument, decades before. He still remembered how he had resented the unnecessary lie.

"She meant well, of course. They go to the synagogue, you know ..."

"She invited me in one evening, and we had quite a pleasant chat ..."

"I'd rather not, I said, if you don't mind ..."

Martin knew that his impatience and intolerance were deeply rooted, and were his true feelings for his mother. It did not seem to be the same for his friends and colleagues. For some it seemed as though the umbilical cord had not been broken. Support for the mother was for them not a chore, but a biological necessity. There were, of course, far fewer fathers.

When she had gone, Martin was exhausted by the duty he had performed - and by his own impatience. She never has any real emotion, he thought - except resignation: she fills her life with other things. He remembered moments which contradicted the judgement, but they had been few. She had nursed her husband gently, in his last days, and he supposed that she had nursed them all, devotedly, as babies. Birth, and death, had meant something to her. It was just what happened in between, he thought intolerantly, that meant nothing, that had been her martyrdom.

He wondered whether anything either had said that morning had been true. He remembered his parents' insistence upon fictions, their denial of reality, in everything that counted. In that respect, at least, they had been united. But he and his brother and sister, all three children, had known that they were disunited. They had submerged each other to the point at which a joint façade could be presented, but the children had seen through it. Cruelly, they had dissected what they imagined to be the structure of their parents' emotional lives.

They can't bear to talk about sex, social position, or food, the children had agreed. The first two aversions could be understood; the third was unexpected. Their parents were, presumably, disappointed in their experience of sex, and in their social positions. But why despise food?

It had interested the children, confident of their own normality. Was it that food, like sex and social position, gave the opportunity of extravagance, or was it simply that it had to do with orifices?

"Good, plain food is best," their father had said, while their mother drowned exquisite vegetables from their garden. They did not seem able to use the word 'eat'. 'What will you take?' they would say to a guest.

The idea that their children might have sexual friendships was so obviously unwelcome that all had joined in the conspiracy of silence. When, finally, one or other had presented a possible fiancé or fiancée, the parents had been taken by surprise. But they had quickly discovered their opposition, and presented it callously.

Whose fault was it all, the children had wondered. Their verdicts were simplistic. Sure that the pattern would not be repeated, they had declared them. Mother was frigid, and Father was clumsy, they had concluded. God knows what they went through! They had put it all into the past.

*

Robert and John were at home. It was Sunday morning.

"How was Switzerland?" said Robert.

"Awful," said John. "I did some work. Not enough."

"Well, did you have time for anything else?"

"You mean women?" Robert always called girls 'women'. Perhaps he's right, thought John. Perhaps that's my trouble: I ought to remember that they are women.

"Well yes, there were one or two."

"Well come on. Tell me about them."

"Nothing to tell, really."

"I know you're a dark horse," said Robert. He seemed annoyed.

"There was one, actually, I rather liked. What about you? What about Mary? How's that going?"

"Oh, she's all right. What about that one you rather liked? Will you be seeing her again?"

"I doubt it." They dropped the subject.

"What exactly is wrong with Father? Do you know?" said John.

"Not really. He says it's a bit of minor plumbing. I suppose he's playing it down - for our benefit."

They were quiet for a time. Then John spoke again.

"How do you think they are?"

"You mean ... together?"

Robert seemed not to have thought of the matter before.

"Well," he said, slowly, "... they've never been demonstrative, but they seem to get on well. That's all you expect, surely. You know, it can't be 'fire in the blood' exactly."

Both were silent, contemplating the unimaginable, what must come to them in a century or two.

"Do you think they'll always want to live here?"

"It would be a huge house - just for them. I know they're sentimental about it."

"Of course, they like seeing us occasionally on Sundays. We'd better keep that up a bit longer."

"I can see it winding up eventually. I suppose Mother'd be upset."

They greeted Martin cheerfully as he came in. "How are you, Dad?" said Robert. "Mother says you've seen a specialist."

"I'm pretty good, Robert. Taking pills of course. Otherwise normal. I'm taking things easily for a time."

Martin poured drinks.

"I thought you'd be bringing Mary," he went on. "Haven't seen her for some time."

"I'll bring her, Dad," said Robert. He turned to John. "John says Switzerland was awful."

"That's what he told us," said Martin. "But I'm sure he's opened his books at least."

"Yes, Dad. I've turned over the pages. Some of them, anyhow."

He did not seem to want to talk about it. Martin noted, again, how rarely his children volunteered truths about their lives. There was no secretiveness, and under questioning, it would come out. Surely I wasn't like that, he thought. So he gave them the benefit of the doubt, and rarely questioned.

"You always talk like that, John. Fortunately, I've learnt to make allowances for it."

"Good old Dad," said Robert.

He paused, then went on.

"Dad, do you think Mother ought to take a job?"

"Ought! Why ought she?"

"Well, you know, in six months or so there may be no-one at home except you and Edward. I know she goes to classes ... and that sort of thing, but everyone says that mothers get a bit lost when the family goes ..."

"I wouldn't worry, Robert. She's well on top of things - quite capable of making decisions, or changing course."

"Father gave a lovely lecture," said Madge, at lunch.

"I was doped, of course," said Martin. "Probably improved it!"

"Anyhow," Madge went on, "it was lovely. I didn't understand a word, but I could tell."

"What about the medal, Dad?" said Joan. "Can we see it?"

"If you must, Joan. I'll get it out."

"I must say, Joanie," said Robert, "that you look most extraordinarily healthy. Sailing must be good for you."

"It is, Robert."

"And how's Steve?" "Just watch, after lunch, and you'll see. We're having our traditional walk in the park."

"Ah, spotty youth returns ..."

"He's not a spotty youth," said Madge. "He's a nice boy."

"I do admire the way you stick up for our boyfriends - and girlfriends," said Robert.

"It's a reaction, Robert," said Martin. "Our parents couldn't bring themselves to recognise that there *were* sexes. You could *see* them switch off if the suggestion arose. It's hard to believe. After all, it is only a generation back, and sex has been going a long time, one way or other."

"Surely," said John, "not all our grandparents! Four of them? Didn't one of them ..."

"They weren't all the same. But ... as you know, there were little irregularities between Mother and me at first, and you could see them refusing to admit anything. And when it became regular, what relief on all sides!"

All were amused.

"I saw my mother yesterday," Martin went on. "I couldn't help remembering all that."

"Were you nice to her, Dad?" said Joan.

"I did my best, Joan."

"I've heard," said Madge, "that it's the other way round now. That it's the young who don't recognise that there are sexes. And their parents make too big a thing of it."

"Never bothered me," said Robert. They laughed.

"What, exactly, never bothered you?" said Joan. Robert stuck out his tongue.

"How's the oboe, Edward," he said. "Are you getting on any better with your reed?"

"An oboe has *two* reeds, Robert," said Edward.

After lunch, Martin and Madge sat with Joan: she was waiting for Steve.

"You realise, don't you, Dad, you'll have to be a father figure to those kids next door."

"Will I, Joan? I would have thought Tom was pretty good himself."

"Oh, Tom! He's just a low sod. All I can say is, she's well rid of him."

"But Joan, I thought you blamed him for walking out."

"Of course I do, Dad. But just because he's the type who'd walk out she's well rid of him."

"I wouldn't say the fault's all on one side, Joan," said Madge.

"But *he* left *her*, Mother!" She spoke much more severely to her mother.

"I know that, darling ..."

"Any man ... who would leave his wife and children ... for another woman, is just a low sod. What do you think, Father?"

"But darling," said Madge, "what if the situation was impossible between them? She couldn't leave him because she'd have nowhere to go - at least not with the children. So he would have to be the one to go."

"They ought to have made it up ... for the sake of the children. Don't you think so, Father?"

"What if they couldn't," said Madge. "Can you always make it up when you've quarrelled with someone?"

"Yes, but he *married* her," said Joan, with finality. "He shouldn't have done it if he couldn't get on with her."

They were quiet for some moments.

"Ah, here's Steve," said Martin.

They watched as Steve and Joan walked out toward the park. Steve was much taller than Joan. Awkwardly, he put his arm around her shoulders.

"I sometimes wonder about Joan," said Madge. "She does seem a bit stiff with boys. What do you think?"

They continued to watch: after some time they saw Joan put her arm around Steve's waist. It was done stiffly.

"I don't think there's anything to worry about," said Martin. "She seems to be very fond of him."

They talked about the children and their worlds. Approaching her examinations, Joan seemed to be remarkably cool. "She has quite a cool streak," said Martin. "Seems to put things in their place."

They were not so sure about John. "He could come a cropper," he said. "Let's hope not."

There was nothing new to be said or thought about Robert:

they knew too little about him. The tortured, reassuring sound of Edward's oboe came down the stairs.

"I suppose ... do you think it's time we had your mother, Martin?"

He turned his mind to the matter. They saw Roy coming up the path: he was carrying gramophone records. Martin rose to open the door.

"I suppose we'd better," he said.

X

As Liz was clearing breakfast, her daughter Helen burst into the room. She was fourteen, and slightly plain. At once Liz put an arm around her.

"Darling! What's the matter? Why aren't you at school?"

Helen pulled herself away. "I can't bear it, Mother. You've no idea how awful it is to be with people you don't want to be with."

"But Helen, it isn't that bad, surely?"

"You just think I'm silly. You just don't know ..."

"I don't think you're silly at all. I know that ... at your age ... things can sometimes seem to be absolutely horrid."

"There you go! *'Seem'* horrid. *'At my age'*. You just don't understand *anything* ..."

Helen burst into tears and ran out of the room, and upstairs.

It had happened before. Liz knew that she must wait for a time. In about half-an-hour Helen came down. She was white-faced and impassive; she had gathered her courage, at great cost.

"Will you give me a note, Mother?"

"Of course I will, darling."

They embraced awkwardly.

Standing at the window, looking toward the forest, Liz hoped Martin would ring.

The telephone rang; she went to it eagerly.

"Hello!"

There was no answer. She spoke her number and waited. There was still no sound. If there was a caller, he was still there. Annoyed, but anxious too, she put down her receiver. She looked at the clock: it stood at half-past ten.

She waited for half-an-hour. The telephone rang again.

"Hello!"

"Hello, Liz."

"Oh darling, I did want you to ring. Did you ring before? Half-an-hour ago?"

"No. You know I only ring at eleven. It's been on my mind. We didn't talk about the hospital business. I've felt guilty about it. I haven't helped you at all."

"Don't feel guilty. I still don't want to talk about it. I just want to see you."

He said nothing, waiting for her to go on.

"It's always the same. About a week after seeing you I can't bear it that we aren't together. I can't bear it now. If I get over that it fades away slowly. About ten days after seeing you I can just about bear it. Then when I know I'm going to see you it gets worse again."

"But Liz..."

"I can't bear it now. Why can't we just be together? Come and live with me. In a caravan! Anywhere!"

"What happened, Liz?"

"It's Helen. She didn't go to school again. She has now, of course. She always does. But it upset me. It's so destructive that she's unhappy. It's because of the other thing, I know. It's because, in my marriage, neither of us is trying. I can't tell you how awful that is. Of course, there's no point in trying now. Because of you. But we'd stopped trying before that. I suppose we started by hoping ... it would get better."

"I know, Liz. It's the same all over the world - everyone hoping for a miracle: that things will be better in the new house, or after the children have gone back to school, or when the *au pair* girl arrives, or the washing machine ... or the bigger bed, or the twin beds, or the separate rooms."

"Can't we meet today, somehow? Haven't you any time?"

"I've a meeting. If it doesn't go on too long I might ..."

"He's so withdrawn. Inhuman almost."

"I'll ring you later, Liz. Will you be there? About half-past twelve."

"Yes, darling, if you can, please."

"You *know* we can't live together," said Martin. "Remember? We agreed about that; we've *adjusted* to it. But I'm only half alive too."

"I know, Martin. I'm just angry. I expect it's because all our neighbours seem to be breaking up. Why shouldn't I?"

"That's funny. Our neighbours seem to be breaking up too."

"I sometimes wish he'd stray a bit. Then at least it wouldn't be me who'd done it to Helen. That's what I want when I'm desperate. Then I think I wouldn't really want it because it would have the same result. Anyway, what a hope!"

"I know, Liz. I sometimes wish Madge would." By his tone he, too, exposed the absurdity of the idea. "As a matter of fact, I used to think sometimes she might have some *chap*. I'll have to go. I'll try to ring again."

She did not reply at once.

"I'm no use to you, Martin. I've told you before. What you need is a full-blooded affair with some nice woman ..."

He interrupted angrily. "I hate you when you say that."

"But," she said, patiently, "even if we did live together, how do we know it would work? I'd turn out to be spoilt. I'd complain because there wasn't enough money."

"I don't think that, Liz. I'd probably turn out to be dull. But we do know what to give ... what to put into it. Surely we could never reach the point ..."

"Above all, Martin, it would be fun! Oh, what fun ... to go out together ... to come back together. To be silly together, even. We'd have rows - noisy, angry rows."

She paused, but went on again.

"It's occurred to me ... about him ... *we* don't seem to have rows."

"That's funny. We don't have rows either. Not now, anyhow."

"Of course," she said, "we don't really have anything."

She paused again.

"Well no, that's not quite true. We have a sort of ... As a matter of fact, I suppose I wouldn't actually leave him. He does seem to need me, in a way - just like Helen. But there's no ..."

Her mood changed suddenly, and she spoke again as though in desperation. "If I don't see you at least every week it isn't worth going on. I might as well stay in my ... golden cage."

She stopped, remembering what she had said earlier.

"'Week!' That's just the worst possible ... oh, it's no good at all, Martin."

"Liz ... I'll ring you. I'll be late for my meeting."

"Of course, darling. Sorry!"

But he did not ring off, and she spoke again.

"Couldn't it sometimes be, not the Strand Palace, or the forest, *please*? Why don't we have a caravan in Croydon? It's half way. Just to be dry and warm, and in our own place. Other people seem to have them ..."

"They're building workers, Liz. Or something like that. We'd have to get planning permission."

Both laughed. His secretary had come in and stood, anxiously, reminding him of his meeting: he must not let her down by being late.

Later, they sat in a pub. In an alcove, their hands touching on a table, they seemed relaxed and happy again.

"What a battlefield!" he said. "Look at them." They looked around the alcoves. "Husbands without wives, and wives without husbands."

"Are you sure?"

"But look! Just look at them. They're *engrossed* in each other. They can't be married!"

Against the bar, and on the floor, the unpolarised young shouted gaily, disposing of the day's absurdities.

"I suppose, on the average," said Liz, "there are more husbands here than wives. How unfair! I'm the lucky exception."

"When we're together, Liz, and touching," - he moved his hand, which still touched hers - "it's possible to be gay about it all. It's even fun - synchronising our watches and all that. Now, with quartz, we can do it to the second."

"Yes, I know. There's some satisfaction even in the *arrangements* of an affair: the deception perfectly accomplished - the efficiency of it. Quite a lot of my women friends talk about that."

"I don't, as a matter of fact," she went on. "It's too serious. It's terrifying if the phone goes when he's there and I think it might be you. It's like a fire engine in the house. Once, I did talk to you when he was there, in another room. I knew he'd say, 'who was that?' I had to go on talking to give myself time to think of an answer."

"I know. There are quite a few things one has to learn. Like remembering the alibis you've used. Otherwise she'll say, one day: 'I was *sure* you said you'd seen Gotsowsky'!"

"How odd," he went on, "that it's the universal theme for farce. People must feel the terror very deeply."

"But it's not being caught in bed that's the terror. Or saying that you were somewhere that turns out to be burnt down. Not even speaking your lover's name in your sleep. It's some absolutely tiny thing that gives it away."

"Like this," said Martin. "A tells his lover B a joke, which she tells A's wife C, forgetting who had told her. But C knows that A knows it. So it must have come from him, and *that* degree of intimacy exists between them."

"Or this," said Liz. "Someone finds a *tiny* piece of torn paper on the floor. He - or she - knows at once: the only thing that has to be torn into such small pieces is an illicit letter. His wife - or her husband - had meant to carry them to the fire, or the waste bin, and had dropped one."

"Here's another. I've heard it's often done. Freud would understand. You mean to ring your lover, but dial your home. When your spouse answers you're thrown for a moment and say something absolutely silly. She - or he - knows you wouldn't have rung up to say that. And of course, if you do happen to have a reversible tie, make sure it's the same way round when you get home as when you left."

"You know how friends meeting at parties hug and kiss each other. Well sometimes you see a pair very obviously *not* doing it when they should. It's a sure sign: I've seen it. As a matter of fact, the only safe lover, they all say, is one whose existence is quite unknown to your husband - as a person. Then you don't give it away by the way you talk about him, or want to talk about him, or want not to. But it's not only terror. They - we - have guilts too. I do. You do, I know."

He waited for her to go on.

"The first is the worst. Twenty-four hours of enormous guilt. When you've had that, it's much easier. And not only easier. Even something to be proud of. And another thing: it's less if it's out-of-doors."

Both smiled.

"And I half believe it's washed away each month."

He touched her hand again. "Without it," she went on, "... adultery, I mean, life wouldn't be worth living. The seventh commandment is absolutely misconceived. And the funny thing is, I'm completely monogamous. I just want one man. When we're together, I don't even dream that he might stray. I think we can just go on as we are."

She looked at her watch. "Darling, I must go. We're giving one of our dinners. It's a judge and his wife this time."

"Shouldn't you be there already, mixing the dressing, or tossing the salad, or something?" There was a faint irony in his voice.

"Oh no," she said, a faint irony in her voice too. "My staff are at it. I just check up before it begins. You should see us: the successful doctor and his attractive, *loyal* wife. Everyone is supposed to think: I wonder how much his success is due to her support. Actually they think: I wonder if she'd make an exception in my case. I wish you could see us."

She stopped.

"No, I don't. I'd hate you to see us. You'd hate it ..."

He interrupted, taking her hand.

"Liz, why *don't* we have a caravan? I was thinking about it in my meeting. Somewhere absolutely anonymous - and accessible. It could be Croydon! I'll look into it."

It had occurred to him that by comparison with the tasks of his professional life it would be a minute project. He had planned projects a thousand times larger. How absurd that he had not thought of it before! He had only to turn his mind to it.

"You're serious, Martin!"

"Of course I am. Of *course* we can do it. What's to stop us?"

The matter was settled. She was delighted; she loved the excitement of the idea, the possibility of change, and of progress.

"What shall we do there?" she said. "Apart from the obvious. What shall we *have* there?" It now lay somewhere between fantasy and reality.

"Well of course, it won't be large, but let's make it reasonably large. You know, a 'mobile home', not a tourer."

"What *do* men have? Penknives, cameras, power tools, pipes ..."

"I think ... what I'd actually like would be a small bench, and a *vice*. I've often fancied doing small repairs, on clocks perhaps, or woodwind instruments - oboes, that sort of thing. Edward's is always going wrong. It's very satisfying. I envy people whose work is real, and mentally contained."

"Well, what I'd like would be a built-in fridge, and a sewing basket. As you know, I'm under-extended as a housewife, and I actually like the housewifely arts. I'd cook, we'd have just enough wine to keep us sober. I'd pull off your buttons and sew them on again. And then ... off to our duties. Me home, to prepare for him, you to your committee ... or whatever it was."

"I think we must go. I'll ring you."

"Tomorrow?"

"Of course."

"You'll see it happens, won't you, Martin?"

"I'll start at once." They were both excited at the new turn. He remembered suddenly that they had still not talked about her illness; he was surprised to realise that he had told her nothing about his own. I can't really think it very important, he thought. Neither of us can.

*

Their talk about guilts had been light-hearted. Time had eroded his memory of the reality. At the start of their affair his own guilts had been anguished. He had thought the word: it was the only one, though he had mocked it in the translations of *lieder* verses and *libretti*. It was not the physical infidelity, but the thought that it was a theft, and the proliferation of minor deceits, which had shamed him.

He had often plotted the course of their affair, reflecting upon its inevitability. He had known Liz, distantly, for years before it began. In their circles there were bands of close acquaintances and bands of distant acquaintances. People moved from one band to another through the chance opportunities of parties and professional encounters. It had surprised him that one who had been, for years, a mere acquaintance, could, quite quickly, become a lover. But he had had only to look back into his youth to remember: it was not the touching of a particular nerve, but the recognition that it had happened to both, that had begun his love affairs. So it could happen suddenly, and without warning. If both wished it, it would grow quickly. Married to Madge, he had assumed that it would not - need not - happen again; he had, indeed, not considered the matter, not known that he wanted it.

One day, having met Liz the day before at a party, he had awoken with a new emotion, long unfamiliar, which he could not define, and whose source he could not at first identify. He knew only that something was changed. It took him minutes to know that his subconscious mind had registered the fact that he had a mild attack of love. It was a physical presence - as he had read somewhere, a light pressure in the chest, as though applied by a screw, or a sort of quiet effervescence. It remained throughout the day, and for several days. When he noticed it, and remembered its cause, he paused to savour it, weighing the words he and Liz had exchanged at the party. They had been serious, not frivolous; innocent, and not flirtatious.

He knew that what had moved him most, what had lodged in his subconsious mind, had been a tiny physical act. As Liz had said, embraces and kisses, physical gestures of a certain kind, were commonplace in the bands of acquaintanceship which they occupied. At a party a male guest would embrace his hostess - and his wife her host - twice exactly. The embraces registered gender without asserting it, and meant 'lovely to see you' and 'lovely party'. Some of their friends used touch as an aid to conversation: all knew it meant nothing, or need mean nothing; others used touch experimentally, questing for opportunity - it could be ignored, or responded to.

Liz, during their conversation, had softly touched his arm once: it signified that a sympathy had been revealed in their talk. He could not now remember what they had talked about, but he still remembered the physical act.

It was strange how revealing such encounters could be, even between strangers. It must be because one could talk, at the same time, both impersonally and intimately: it was, so to speak, theoretical, as though about third persons. One could talk about oneself, or even about one's marriage partner - it would hardly be disloyal. And there were no forbidden areas, as grew in a marriage. So the encounters were more significant - and more dangerous - than might be supposed. Perhaps that was their purpose.

If it happened that the two became lovers their talk would move, almost without changing, into lovers' talk - with its own excitements and lack of inhibition: the groundwork had been done. It was the discovery of common sympathies and attitudes which excited - which was the true occasion of the love affair, and it was the lack of forbidden areas which freed one from inhibition. 'You're the only one I could have said that to', one might say. They would talk less about their spouses: it was not only tactless, but almost irrelevant. It was also unfair, because the spouses could not retaliate.

But of course, it was not the whole story. It was also newness which excited. Martin had heard that for some it was the only excitement. The newness of the lover's touch did too: the slightest touch, experimental perhaps, meant more than the informed, experienced touch of the partner. Talk and touch fed upon each other as the affair grew. It was almost the mirror image of the decline of a marriage, where the failure of one destroyed the other. He had experienced both in his love affair and marriage with Madge. It seemed, indeed, that most of the human race had been deceived by the first and surprised by the second.

Some days later Martin had asked Liz to lunch with him. He did not tell Madge, had not yet made up his mind whether he would do so after the event, or pretended that he had not. He had kept it at a distance.

In the course of his conversation he said: "I'm very much afraid that I'm becoming susceptible to you". It was his gesture, his complement to hers at their previous meeting. As he said it he remembered another discovery of his youth: he had always been as much moved by his own gestures as by the girl's.

She smiled, making fun of him. "On a scale of 1 to 10," she said, "*how* susceptible are you?"

"About three-and-a-half," he said.

She had smiled again, but this time it was a new kind of smile. She had shown, not her teeth, but her mouth. She had seemed to open herself to him: he knew that he was captured.

That evening, uncertain how to face Madge, he found himself looking, very directly, into her eyes. Did he want to give her the opportunity of finding him out? Or was he testing his power to deceive her? He could not be sure. She seemed to see nothing. He had sat with her, silently cataloguing the possibilities.

'We only talk', he might say. It was disingenuous. Disloyalty began as soon as one had a conversation with a woman which one would not have with one's wife, or would not want her to hear. Nothing was more intimate.

But could he not be allowed an *understanding*, an added richness in his life, going no further, and without prejudice or hurt to his marriage? Was he not entitled to that degree of disloyalty?

Or could it not be moderated to a point *below* the level of danger? Was there no safe plateau? Could they now, somehow, discover a *formula* which would be fair to all?

He was not deceived. He had found, absurdly, that he already missed Liz's presence: it was a kind of homesickness; he had not remembered that feeling. It was the reality which that signified which could hardly be denied, refused, or moderated. There *was* no safe plateau. He suspected already that the answers to his questions were negative: that he would not stop; that he would not tell Madge; that - as most of his friends and colleagues seemed to have done - he would embark on an affair, on faithlessness; that there would be deception, self-contempt, perhaps discovery. He was not practised in deception, could not tell whether he would be good at it. It had, he knew, already begun: it did not require a spoken lie, only a failure of truth. He did not know what effect it might have on his marriage: it must surely destroy the reality of his own part in it. Was it not the same for all those others, those millions? Had they not all thought the same thoughts? Had they not all hoped to discover the formula?

He had seen Madge looking at him with enquiry: she must have recognised an unfamiliar mien. He set about a return to normality, his new face already a little practised.

He had resisted temptation for some days, fractionally hoping that it might go away, gingerly testing himself. In his youth he had fallen in love quickly, out of love - when that became necessary - slowly. He found that he had not changed. Again he felt the strange homesickness, the wish to recall everything he and Liz had said to each other - almost speaking the words again, almost wallowing in them - the lift of his spirit when he thought he might see her again, and her smile.

By two physical gestures she had captured him. And yet, he had hardly noticed her physical self, could not have said for certain whether she was beautiful.

At their next meeting he told her about the light pressure in his chest.

"There?" she said.

"No, a little lower."

He kissed her; she groaned quietly. Surely the matter was sealed! They would not walk into an affair - as it were - backwards, not seeing it, protesting that it was not to happen, pretending that it was not happening; they would jump straight in. He knew that her person, and her unknown body, would turn into instruments of sympathy; that his desire for her would grow, that he would see to it that it overruled his guilts, anguished though they might be.

Quite soon they had met again: this time it was she who was hesitant.

"What do you want out of this affair?" she said.

"Victory," he said. That pleased her. She smiled, again showing her mouth. He saw that she was indeed beautiful, and that it was her mouth that showed it.

XI

"Have we ever actually met Marjorie?" said Madge.

"I don't think so," said Martin. They were walking to Marjorie's flat. Tom had invited them to dinner, and to meet her. "We've seen her around, of course."

"How nice to see you, Martin ... Madge," said Tom, as they arrived. "How nice of you to come."

He seemed to be a little more extrovert than was normal for him, a little louder. He and Madge kissed.

"Do meet Marjorie. These are my old friends - Martin and Madge Blake."

Ah, thought Martin: not to mention we were neighbours.

It was a bed-sitting-room, rather than a flat. A large divan bed stood in one corner; a kitchen hid behind a screen. The bed was inescapable - it dominated the room. It would be hard to deny its presence, to avert one's eye.

"What a nice flat, Marjorie," said Martin. He and Madge looked around it eagerly, admiring the books, and the wall-hangings. They went to the window and looked out. A table, laid for four, stood in an alcove. Tom's possessions, if he had any there, had so far made no impact: it was still a feminine room.

"We're hoping to get a bigger flat, of course," said Tom. "I really need a study, and Marjorie needs a proper studio."

"Where are you looking, Tom?"

"Oh, we'd like to stay around here, wouldn't we, Marjorie."

"It's handy for us both," said Marjorie. "But they're not easy to come by ... and rather expensive."

"We went to agents on Saturday," said Tom. "They're lining up a few for us to see."

He poured drinks.

"That's some of Marjorie's work." Tom pointed to the wall-hangings.

"You're very clever, Marjorie," said Madge. "I wish I could do things like that."

"I'm sure you could, Madge."

"She's very modest," said Tom. "She always is about her own work. But they really are ... rather good. I'm very proud of her."

Marjorie laughed. "I'll have to see to the dinner." She went behind the screen.

"Tell me when you need me, Marjorie," said Tom.

"Well, Tom," said Martin. "How's the job?"

"The usual panic. Everything to be changed one day, back where we were next day. No wonder income tax is where it is."

Tom looked harassed. The Government - and the nation - as well as Deirdre, had always harassed him. He had usually seemed to have a particular complaint, had expounded it, and his remedy, at length. Quite soon, he launched himself. His views had always seemed to Martin to be eccentric - the views of one in the know, discreet of course, and bearing no relation to the political scene as apparent to the ordinary world.

He worked himself up, naming no-one, taking no political position, but displaying it nakedly. If he had not been a civil servant, thought Martin, he could have been quite a politician.

Tom stopped suddenly, grinning as he realised that he had been performing.

"How's it going, Marjorie?"

"All right, Tom. Perhaps you could come and carve, and would you sit at the table, Martin ... Madge ..."

They went to the table. A bottle of wine stood on it. "Shall I open the bottle, Tom?" said Martin.

"Yes, if you would, Martin." Marjorie brought out four plates with the carved meat.

"It was a delicious meal," said Martin later, "we really must ..." He stopped.

"We must fix something up."

"And we have enjoyed meeting you, Marjorie," said Madge. "I'd like to talk to you again ... about those hangings."

"Oh, do! Perhaps ... when the men are busy ... we could ..."

"What a good idea."

"How old would you say she is?" said Martin, as they walked

home. "Thirty ... three ... five?"

"It's hard to say. She could be more. She's definitely not twenty-eight."

"She could have been married before. On the whole ... I'd guess not."

"There is that bed, of course."

They were quiet for a time.

"Do you think ... I mean ... do they go together?" said Madge.

"Not really. They don't seem to have a mutual personality. Not yet, anyhow."

"Of course, we didn't actually find out anything about her."

"No ... and none of us said a word about ... anything."

"All they wanted was respectability - a dull, married conversation. He's hoping to join the respectable again with Marjorie. It'll be quite a long haul."

After a pause he spoke again, not seriously, but not quite unserious.

"I wonder if one could set up as a marriage assessor. You know, couples would come and show themselves, pay their fee, and have one's expert opinion on whether to get married."

She was amused. "How would you do it?"

"Well ... you'd look at their physical make-up, sexiness, their sizes, aggressiveness, temperaments ..."

"Isn't it the pecking order ... sexual pecking order we've talked about before?"

"I suppose it is."

"What about interests, education ..."

"Secondary, I should think, Madge."

He stopped and thought for a moment.

"I wonder if he smokes his pipe now."

*

Martin and Madge had again met Jim and Alice in a pub. Jim was cheerful, Alice a little anxious: she thought he was drinking too much; they had arrived first. But it was near home for all four, and all knew it would be a particular kind of evening: friendship would be augmented, and inhibitions loosened, by drink.

"I've another idea for a play," said Jim, when all had drinks. "Funny, this time, with serious undertones, of course. It could be called 'The Bell' - if that hadn't been used." Alice smiled: she had heard it before.

"Apparently straight adultery is out ... for the time being. There's a log jam of those. Sensitive, humorous plays in the same area are in. So I have this couple going through a sticky patch: they can't help getting into rows. Well one day he brings home a hand-bell and proposes that when it is rung, by either, he - or she, of course - has the right to an uninterrupted exposition of his point of view, of whatever they are rowing about. Next day *she* brings home a motor horn, and proposed that whoever honks it has the right, without later recrimination, to lose his temper - or hers, of course - and work right through *that*. Then they bring other devices - a gong, perhaps, or a drum; sounding any one gives the right to do something which he couldn't normally get away with."

"That's as far as he's got," said Alice.

"Well, I admit I'm stuck. I don't know what happens in the middle. But I know what happens at the end: as the credit titles go up there's a *farrago* of bell-ringing, honking, gonging. What do you think of that?"

"Promising, Jim," said Martin. "Could I interest you in a little invention of mine? Technically quite simple - any of my technicians could make one."

"We didn't, actually, have one," said Madge. She had heard this before.

"In your play," Martin went on, "there's nothing about making up. Now you'll agree that it could happen that both would like to make up, but to be the first to say so would be construed as admitting one was wrong in the first place. We'll assume the process usually takes place in bed. So, under each pillow there's an electric bell-push. But the bell doesn't ring until both pushes have been pressed, and only after a delay - half-an-hour, perhaps, or even longer. When it finally rings no-one can be sure who pressed it first. So there's no victory, and no face lost. As long as the bell does ring they can safely make it up ... in any way that's convenient."

Jim seemed to be thinking hard. "Could it be arranged," he said, "that the delay was *variable*, so that neither could know how long it actually was?"

"Of course, Jim. No problem."

"I wonder if I could use it: build it in with the other bells. May I have it, Martin?"

"Of course you may."

"I'll buy you a drink for the copyright."

"Have you ever noticed," said Jim later, "how absolutely marvellous pub conversations are, when you can't quite hear everything?"

He lowered his voice.

"There are two near us. Both would make marvellous plays. I wish I could just put it straight down."

"Just as they are, Jim?" said Martin. "You mean with *gaps* when you can't hear?"

"Of course, Martin. When you can't hear it's because someone has lowered his voice. So you miss all the crucial bits." He seemed excited.

"There he goes again," said Alice. "He just won't put down the crucial bits. We have to imagine them."

"Well of course, Alice. That's the whole point."

He stopped, as though listening. Nearby a couple, working-class, middle-aged, a little decrepit, and fairly drunk - were performing. Only occasional sentences could be heard. The four listened, looking at each other, not at the couple.

"If and when he goes ..." said the woman. She lapsed into inaudibility.

Later the man intervened. "Don't you worry," he said. "I'll sort it out." He rose and walked unsteadily to the counter, returned with two drinks.

Quietly, just audibly, he said: "Don't forget, my dear, I'd do anything for you." Now he too lapsed into inaudibility.

"I don't owe anybody anything," he said later, audibly.

"Of course you don't," said the woman.

The four, still looking at each other, and saying nothing, listened to another couple. They were young, black, obviously American, and sophisticated. Only the man could be heard, and only some of his words. "You're always trying to put me in the position ..." he said. He became inaudible.

The woman answered; they could not hear what she said.

"That's a typically unfair remark," said the man.

"See what I mean?" said Jim, as though their own conversation had not stopped.

"I do," said Madge. "How sad for them! They're such a long way from home."

"It does seem to be mostly about one thing - or at least in one area," said Alice.

"Well," said Jim, "granted that there is only one area, you've just seen my artistic battlefield. How much do I put down, and how much do I leave out? Knowing what's there, of course, as everyone else is supposed to."

"Why do you always have to make us work?" said Alice.

"Another part of it," he went on, a little bitterly, "is how good can I *afford* to make it."

Again Alice reached her hand toward him. He seemed excited by his own enthusiasm.

"It's a variation of the Ibsen thing - public image turning out to have been quite wrong, quite different from reality. But I want to build the reality slowly, with only little bits of image here and there."

"Is there a reality?" said Martin. "Or rather, don't most of us have an image as well as a reality?"

"Don't most of us fluctuate?" said Madge. "You know - sometimes we're nice people, sometimes we're not."

Jim seemed to be thoughtful. "You may be right."

"Back to the drawing board, then," said Alice.

They all laughed.

Martin and Madge, walking home, talked about their friends.

"She seems very affectionate," said Martin.

"He's very good value," said Madge.

"It was a nice evening. Jolly, even. We didn't once mention their crack. I think they were both relieved."

"They're nice friends. They don't seem to mind that we're older than they are."

"No, that is nice." They were quiet for a time.

"How do you think they are, Madge? I mean, do you think they're getting on any better?"

"Isn't it hard to say! But there is a kind of *unity* about them."

"Yes. One feels that if they do ever ... split up, it'll be very anguished - on both sides."

"Isn't it always anguished, Martin? Wouldn't it have been anguished if we split up?"

"I'm sure it would, Madge. But why ... did you ever think that we might?"

She answered quickly, as though there was no need to think about the answer. "Not seriously, Martin. No, I don't suppose I have."

"I don't suppose I have either. Not seriously. Of course, we used to row a lot. We didn't seem to have the knack of defusing. We always seemed to be fusing."

Until, he thought, we turned half away from each other.

"Isn't it odd," she said, "how Jim and Alice - and all of us - can talk and laugh about it, but it's desperately serious."

"His story is right to the point, actually."

"So is yours - about the bell-push."

"The point being, I suppose, that no-one wants to admit ... at such times ... that he was wrong."

"Isn't it because ... at such times ... one hates and despises the other. To admit one was wrong is to abase oneself before someone one despises. No-one can bear that."

"Another thing: no-one can bear the idea that he's been so stupid, so careless, as to link himself - for ever - with someone he despises."

"Exactly! But even when there isn't any row one still expects - for one's own self-respect - too much from the other. When it doesn't come one tries to make it come - to change him, to make him do whatever you want him to."

"The funny thing is ... it probably turns out to be exactly what he'd always thought he'd been most careful to do. Or she, of course."

"Perhaps," she said, "if one of us had thought about splitting up, he - or she - would have assumed the other wouldn't want to."

"I expect you're right, Madge."

They had reached their home.

"Why did you buy a caravanning magazine, Martin? I saw it in your room. Are you thinking of that sort of holiday?"

"Not really. Just the usual thirst, at the bookstall, for something to read."

In the hall, she remembered something. "You won't forget Edward's speech day, will you? You know he's performing."

"Of course not, Madge." He took out his diary. It was, indeed, unthinkable that either parent should fail in this duty.

*

At the speech day Martin and Madge sat with other parents, regressed, turned into schoolchildren themselves, doing as they were told, receiving what the Headmaster, the Chairman, and the distinguished visitor wished them to hear. They despised the assumptions and procedures of the occasion, but contained themselves.

Edward, too, despised the occasion. But he would have been shocked if his parents had not come, or if they had shamed him by unconventional action or dress.

With practised confidence the speakers presented their idealised picture of the school, and the world. The school was, indeed, a microcosm. Like the world, it contained no problem which could not be solved by common sense and sound values - which the vast majority of the school's population possessed. Those who did not were no real danger: they could, of course, go elsewhere. Martin and Madge looked at each other with embarrassment and apology as the contentious was turned into the incontrovertible.

Quite quickly the Headmaster moved to safe ground. "Now we have music for you. We are very proud of what Mr Fisher does for our boys, and I am sure you will be too."

The parents settled, as they had done every year, to hear the offerings of talent or of tortured instruction. It now appeared that music, not education, or the inculcation of values, must have been the aim of the school year.

Parents whose sons were to perform became nervous. When Edward, the youngest and most precarious performer of a wind quintet, played Mozart, Martin and Madge hung anxiously on every note. They applauded without reserve as the five boys, relieved that it had not been too bad, bowed and smiled.

He's really quite fragile still, thought Martin. I hope he'll be all right.

He's only a boy, thought Madge: not even adolescent.

Afterwards the parents were free to wander through the school, to meet the teachers and Headmaster, and to have tea.

"Ah, Professor and Mrs Blake," said the Headmaster, "so nice to see you. We're very proud of Edward. I'm told he's making real progress on the oboe." He beamed at them with pride and gratification.

XII

What had sustained Madge, through the months of early summer, was her certainty that she would not see Patrick again. In their previous wars the hard thing had been the daily affirmation of any decision. Wars between lovers were wars of attrition: one would be starved into surrender, into accepting the terms laid down by the other.

This time she had accepted that her own decision was final, and waited, in pain, only for the pain to lessen. The attrition had been of herself. She had not wanted him to make an approach: it would have only delayed her cure.

But it had not been straighforward. At times she boasted to herself that she was recovering, would begin to feel almost happy. At other times she wondered whether it was even possible to recover.

Her days in Brighton, and the small house, had given her a small core, and a taste of freedom. She was her own person, a character in a novel, and something might happen. But in the end these had served only to point what she had lost.

It was unthinkable that she could go into the summer, and into the years ahead, without some of that excitement and adventure, that indescribable emotion. Even if advancing age reduced the need for them, or the capability - and she doubted it - she was not willing to wait for that.

Bitterly, and ironically, she contemplated the falseness of her life. She wondered how common was such entire alienation, such disparity between image and reality. Of course, one knew of family disasters - was surrounded by them - but surely it was abnormal to be quite so dangerously poised, and for so long.

As the summer approached, and the violent ending of her affair receded, she found herself beginning to argue the matter again.

If he had been definitely committed to the other, she thought, that would be different: it would be inevitable, and easier to bear. Or if he had pushed me away. But he didn't. I couldn't stand that he wasn't committed to me, so I pushed him away.

She knew, but would not admit it to herself, that by arguing the matter, by admitting the possibility that she might, indeed, see him, she had decided that she would.

At times she argued that all she wanted was to see him, so to speak, for old times' sake - to see how he was, to exchange, harmlessly, reminiscences of their friendship, to reinstate at least that part of their relationship. She knew it was not true.

I'm weakening, she thought, after all this time! It'll be back to the beginning, then through it all again. The thought terrified but excited her: the temptation grew to be enfolded, once more, and to feel his weight on her.

"Madge, how lovely to hear you!"

"Why haven't you rung me?" It was a flimsy device, and absurd after so many months, but she needed it. She did not give him time to answer.

"How are you, Patrick?"

"I'm fine, Madge. How are you?"

"I'm fine, Patrick."

They talked gaily. She was suddenly happy: the memory, and shame, of their last meeting, were, by agreement, to be erased; the months of pain were to be forgotten.

"When am I going to see you?" he said, later.

She paused for a moment, as though surprised.

"Yes, I'd like that. Why don't we meet?"

"This week?"

In her euphoria she thought, suddenly: I'll take him to my house.

"Can you make Thursday?"

It had always been Thursday, of course; she knew he could make himself free on that day. But he played his part, and hesitated.

"Yes, why not. What shall we do?"

"I'd like to go to Brighton. I've something to show you."

"Really!" He was amused. "All right, Brighton. When shall I pick you up?" .

They arranged their meeting.

"One thing," she said.

He waited.

"No tow-path talk, I promise."

"Of course not, Madge."

It had been their term for the interminable, tortured quarrels they had had, walking up and down, on a tow-path near his flat. Should they, or should they not, continue to see each other? One, always, had argued that they should not; but they had always compromised.

She was buoyant, amazed that she had not thought of it before.

Waiting at the spot arranged, Madge felt again the special excitement - it had hardly diminished since her adolescence - which she had always felt while waiting for a boy, or a man, who was certain to come. The afternoon was both warm and cool.

He drove a sports car, and he had lowered the hood. As soon as they met, she saw in his expression the reflection of hers.

"There's no-one like you, Madge, for putting it all out."

"It's lovely to see you," she said.

They laughed. "That's what it was, on your face," he said. "You looked marvellous."

As they drove through the long sequence of suburbs they talked - about her children, about Martin, about his children, and their mother.

"She's settling down without me. Quite cosily, actually. We're even on speaking terms!"

Holding to her promise, Madge did not ask about the other woman. What a simple rule, she thought. Just keep off that, and everything's O.K.

As soon as they reached the country she put her hand on his thigh. It was a familiar gesture, signifying acceptance, confidence, a need to neutralise the charge between them. They now talked less.

"What a gorgeous day!" she said.

He was a fast driver, and the road encouraged it.

"But why Brighton? And what have you got to show me?"

"Just wait. I promise it isn't anything historic, or even architectural."

He was amused, and delighted, by her house.

"It's mine, actually. Even the family don't know about it."

"Just like you, Madge. But ... who comes here?"

"I come here. So far, only me. Now, it seems, you and I."

She took charge. "It's warm now, but it'll be cold later on, so we'll light the fire. Then we'll walk on the Prom. Then we'll come back and have a meal."

She showed him her larder.

"All in order. I'll get what else we need."

"What about the Prom?" she went on. "Do people here know you? At the University, I mean. I'd like to walk up and down with you."

"Oh ... perhaps one or two. But I doubt whether they'll be walking on the Prom. Anyhow, I'm not even a married man at present. What about you?"

"I'll chance it." It was part of her creed, and he had shown that it was a part of his too. A certain amount of brazenness was necessary to a love affair. Too timid a secrecy was demeaning.

"You light the fire, and I'll check up on everything else," she said. A moment later she came back, and stood in a doorway.

"When we come back, Patrick, I'll have you in *my* bed. I never have. I'll turn everything on."

She switched on the electric blanket and a fan heater in the bedroom. She had not slept in the bed, and had not known when she might do so. But she had bought sheets and blankets, and kept them aired.

Could it be, she thought, that this is what it was all for? But surely I'd have bought a double bed if it had been.

For both, though they were middle-aged, nakedness was significant, and not ridiculous, and though she was modest, and anxious about her breasts, she could easily be reassured. She knelt on the bed in the small room, her back against the wall, covering her breasts with the sheet. He pulled it away.

"It's just as lovely, just as ... awful ..." She passed her hand over his flat stomach. "How do you manage it?"

"The first time you did that," she went on, "... pulled the sheet away, I wrote in my diary one word: 'momentous'. I've still got it. I adore it all."

He folded her underneath him, with his lovely strength and weight.

"Are you going to sleep?" she said.

"You mean ... afterwards ..." he said, quietly. She could not connect his good humour and gentleness with the force and anger he had displayed when they quarrelled. What a fool I was, she thought, to give him up. Just this, just these hours, are enough. As long as I remember that, I can keep him. No tow-path talk. Not even tow-path thoughts.

She lay uncomfortably, but gratefully, trapped half underneath him in the small bed. I'll give him twenty minutes, she thought. Then we'll have a bath. Then I'll make dinner.

A loud knock on the front door roused her; she had nearly fallen asleep. He had awoken and they listened, quietly and tensely, but also amused.

"It's the meter man," she said, whispering.

"It's the Vice-Chancellor," he said, whispering too. "Tracked us down to our Brighton love-nest." They continued to listen. Whoever was at the door was not more than a few feet from them. He knocked again.

"Does anyone live here?" He seemed to be speaking to a neighbour.

"I don't know," said the neighbour. "I've seen someone once or twice. She's not here all the time."

There was silence for a few moments.

"I'd just put it though the letter-box," said the neighbour.

"I'm supposed to find out if anyone lives here first."

They continued to listen. "Just remember that it's England," said Patrick.

The flap of the letter-box rattled; they heard the unknown official walk away. Both laughed, loudly.

She extricated herself and ran into the bathroom, turned on the taps, and came back with the buff-coloured envelope, forcing herself back into the bed.

"It's the Electoral Register!" They laughed again.

"How gorgeously slow everyone is, catching up on me."

"Well," he said, "I decided long ago that I'm far too old to put my trousers on in a hurry."

She knew that the new cycle in her affair had been entered carelessly. Like the Electoral Officer, perhaps Martin would eventually discover her. But by closing a part of her mind she could delight in an uncomplicated present. He seemed to join in her delight.

XIII

"Aren't they gorgeous!" said Madge to Patrick. "Just look." It was a new meeting.

They were on the Downs: each carried a bag. Arm-in-arm, they walked slowly. Every love affair identified places: theirs had been Patrick's flat, and the river banks and tow-path nearby. Now, in a new cycle, she had found new ones for them.

"I wish," she said, "we'd had some way of being outdoors before. If we'd been able to go away - even for a few days - just walking, or camping ..."

"You *are* an outdoor person, Madge. As soon as the sun touches you, you look absolutely marvellous, and your skin ..."

Holding her hand, he raised their two bare arms, showing where they touched.

"Of course, today is perfect," she said. "The sun is exactly right, and the breeze is exactly right. And we'll be back before it turns cold."

"When I was a boy," he said, "I sometimes used to go over the ground before I went out with a girl. I'd find a hollow, or a shelter, and steer towards it."

She was amused. "Did it work?"

"Never. It made me nervous, and the girl saw it. Far better ... to steer by the wind." He put his arm around her waist.

The particular way in which he had always done it, and in which she had received it, had been a resonance for them.

"I wouldn't worry too much about Martin," he said. "If he has to have the operation, it's about four to one on, and that means he only has to be reasonably lucky, and he'll have no more trouble. I asked one of my colleagues. He should be much fitter, actually."

"Four to one! Is that all, Patrick? What happens if it's the ... one?"

"Four to one is good, Madge. It's worth doing at those odds."
She was still anxious. "Would you?"
"No doubt. Like a shot."
"Of course. He wouldn't have any doubts either. You men!"

She had noticed the evasion. "It does make me sad, Patrick. I can't help remembering, once - we were sitting on a beach. Martin was tossing pebbles slowly; he seemed very thoughtful. Then he said: 'I'm just working out, if someone threw one pebble out of a box every day of his life, how big would the box have to be.' I said something silly, like: 'how can you work that out?' And he said: 'of course I can't work it out exactly. But I can make reasonable assumptions, like, that the pebbles are all exactly round, and all about this size.' I knew I mustn't say that they weren't round. So he went on for a bit, calculating, then he said: 'quite a small bucket.'"

"How is he, Madge? Mentally, I mean."

"What do you mean, Patrick?"

"It's on the grapevine that there's talk of splitting his department. I wondered what he thought of it."

"He hasn't said anything." She was amazed. "I'm sure he'd hate it. He *loves* his department!"

"It's only the grapevine, Madge. Could be quite wrong."

She was thoughtful. "I have wondered whether there was something in the air. Poor old Martin!"

With an effort, Madge closed the two parts of her mind which could destroy the day's happiness. With the arm carrying her bag she pressed Patrick's hand into her waist.

"What a perfect spot!" she said, suddenly, then turned to face him. "Are you sure you haven't been over the ground?" He laughed. It was sheltered, but high, so that it had a view.

She felt the grass: it was dry. Taking charge, she unpacked their picnic. He had brought wine, and coffee in a Thermos flask; she had brought food.

"Our first picnic," she said.

They sipped the wine, drinking each other's health.

"It used to strike me as strange," she said, "that we can talk about Martin, and we always have ..."

"But why not, Madge? This ... us ... has nothing to do with him."

"I know that, Patrick, as it has turned out. But it could have had a lot to do with him. I could have been telling you what a heel he was, and that sort of thing."

"As I know him, that would have been hard to believe. Not impossible, of course. No-one knows anything about anyone else's marriage. He might have been a heel - as a husband."

"Well, as you know, he isn't. Of course, he isn't perfect. Actually he does seem to be a little uninterested in *sex*. Or perhaps it's sublimated. He's absolutely absorbed in his job."

"Ah well, everyone knows that marriage is the one institution into which sex doesn't enter. It's far too dangerous."

She laughed. "I'm sure you've said that before."

She became serious. "As a matter of fact, when I ... when we ..."

"When we started 'going out' together," he said gently. It was a well-known euphemism of teenagers, meaning almost exactly the opposite of what it seemed to mean.

"Yes, Patrick." She smiled. "When we started to go out together I was quite relieved that he seemed to be hardly interested. Funnily enough, we never talked about it. Things just took their course - or rather, didn't."

We still haven't talked about it, she thought with amazement.

"I sometimes wondered whether he worked too hard on purpose."

"We talk about the children too," she went on. "And that could be thought odd."

"Yours mainly, Madge. As I've told you before, you're the most obsessed parent I've ever met."

"Well, I think I'm getting over that. It'll be Martin who'll be trying to keep the family together, trying to get them to come on Sunday - that sort of thing."

She poured more wine into their glasses.

"I love it that we're having a picnic, Patrick. We've never had one before. Couldn't we sometimes do other things? Couldn't we ... go to the theatre, or something like that? Or go out to dinner in London?"

"Of course, Madge! Of course we could."

It's just, she thought, that I don't want it to be only bed ... or tow-path. She wanted to go on talking.

"I used to be surprised how ... different a lover is from a husband. I'm still surprised by it."

"What usually happens, Madge, is that the lover is turned into a spouse. Quite soon you're back where you started. At least that didn't happen to us."

She was a little angry with him. "I wasn't entirely pleased about that, Patrick."

He was unwilling to be serious.

"Lovers are so much more fun, Madge."

"It's much easier to be a lover, Patrick. Especially at first, when it's all ... ascending."

"The change is so slow ... one hardly notices it."

They were quiet for a time. She had prepared the food with care, and had done it at her London home. So she had broken one of her rules.

"Why do I love these Downs so much?" she said. "It's only chalk. Just big curved sweeps of chalk - with a topping of grass, or corn, or whatever it is. Why don't we just walk, some time? Start at Arundel, and walk along the top. Stay in pubs. Go upstairs to bed every night, straight from the bar. Finish at Brighton, bath and become civilised in my house, and back to London."

"You're full of plans, Madge. Why not just ... steer by the wind?"

The sun warmed them gently, and the breeze cooled them gently. "It's perfect," she said.

Later she lay, face downward on the grass. "I might even go to sleep. Just make sure you're touching me, somewhere."

Odd how fidgety I am today, she thought. Nice of him not to say so. The word 'febrile' came into her mind. She wondered what it meant. I'm sure I'm being febrile, she thought. What I'm doing is giving him chances to say something about the future - which he doesn't take - without being explicit about it as I used to be. I must stop it: must stick to our bargain.

If it were not such a perfect day, if it were cold, or raining, today might have been a disaster. And yet, I longed for it all week.

She slept, briefly.

"Madge," she heard him say, "wake up. It's turning cool." He nursed her gently awake. "Why don't we ... not go back to the house, but drive slowly back along the lanes. Find a nice pub if we can."

She was grateful - that he had sensed that that was what she wanted, and that he had excused her from the obligation to make it obvious.

"I'd like that." They walked back to the spot where his car stood, outside a house in an ordinary street. Outside other houses one or two car-owners tended their cars. For them it was an ordinary day.

"They have all that on their doorsteps," he said, "and there was no-one there, except us." Both could see that their use of the street was slightly resented.

As they drove back they talked again.

"We never got near living together, Madge," he said. He spoke gently. "It was your kids, of course. You are the most obsessed parent I've ever met."

"It was usually when one of them was ill, Patrick. I used to be obsessed then. When Joan had glandular fever I thought about nothing else ..."

"You certainly talked about nothing else," he said, still gentle.

"Did I really? I'm sorry. What a bore I must have been."

"Not boring, Madge. But it was a warning to me."

"Warning?"

"Well ..."

He seemed to be uncertain whether to go on.

"Well, you remember - or perhaps you don't - that there were times when I tried to detach you from that family of yours."

"Of course, Patrick. You nearly did."

"I didn't, Madge."

They were quiet for a time.

"Patrick," she said. "When I was with you ... when I *am* with you, it was - still is - total."

"Nearly."

"Nearly?"

"No complaints, Madge. It's total when we were ... are ... together. Even talking about our children seemed very warming; seemed to strengthen it. I didn't know until later that you'd never have left them. And I suppose we both boggled at the idea of adding yours to mine ..."

"I didn't know either, Patrick. I suppose I could have left Martin. He's grown-up. 'All's fair!' But when I began to think what it would mean, putting my ... brood ... through it all ..."

"More than that, Madge. You wouldn't have done *anything* to hurt them. I always knew that ... some time in the evening ... you'd remember something you'd promised to do for one of them ..."

"Oh dear ..."

"How did we get on to all this?" he said, as though angrily. She put her hand on his thigh.

"Then we thought she had meningitis."

"Every parent's nightmare. It turns out to be something else. Eventually she's perfect again. It's only the parents who've been damaged."

"Patrick, what is it actually *like*, being a doctor?"

"Great, at first. Of course you think you deserve it, because it's a bloody long course. The *power* is unbelievable. By a word, or two words, you can change someone's life. 'Forget it,' you say, and he does. Or she does. Everyone thinks he has something wrong with him. Several things. Usually he's right. But you know that some of them don't matter. Later, when you begin to be able to tell, simply by looking at his face, that one of your friends is going to die of cancer, it's not so great."

"Just by looking, Patrick?"

"Yes, Madge. No-one knows whether you're seeing that he has cancer, or that he knows he has cancer. But you see, all right."

*

That evening Joan had called at Bryan's flat. It was the first time she had done it unexpectedly: she had wanted to surprise him.

But Bryan seemed to be a little irritated by her arrival. Shocked, she realised, for the first time, that he had meant their relationship to be narrow, their rôles to be limited. He was to be the older man, and teacher in love; she was to be the young girl, and pupil. Other matters did not enter into his scheme. Her arriving unexpectedly had placed them on an equal basis, had been a violation of the rules.

Seeing that she had noticed it, he quickly adopted his lover's *persona*. He swept his arm around her thighs as she stood above him in a gesture - dismissing her clothing as irrelevant - which she had found unanswerable. Uncertain, but instinctive, she had pushed him away gently and made her visit short. "You're busy, aren't you," she said.

Madge, returning home, saw her fumbling in her school satchel and sobbing a little. At once she burst into tears; she could not restrain them, but wept loudly. Joan heard, and ran to her.

"Whatever's the matter, Mum?" Her own tears stopped; she put her arms around Madge's shoulders.

Madge was incoherent. She was trying to say something.

"It's just ... I saw you crying, and looking into your satchel for something. It's so *awful* ... I don't know why ... just someone looking in a satchel ... and crying ..."

Both were now weeping, and both were incoherent.

"I was only getting out my homework."

Madge's weeping became wilder and louder,

"Homework!"

"Why did you think I was crying?" said Joan, after a time. "It was really nothing, Mum."

Each had her arms around the other; they went on weeping, unashamedly, and finally, cathartically.

"Is it your exams?" Joan shook her head.

"Was it Reginald?"

"Of course not, Mum. He doesn't bother me. He's just a joke. Anyway, I never go through the garages now."

The neighbour whom they knew as Reginald had turned out to be a molester. Joan, coming home from school, had found that she hated to pass across Mr Hutton's main window. He would be there, would greet her with a slight, unsmiling bow. So she had begun to use a short cut which led, through the forecourt of communal garages, to her own back door. But later a new hazard faced her here: Reginald had taken to waiting for her. His molestations had been crude, and she resisted him easily. She was practised in fending off predatory men: it was a necessary part of the technique of modern living.

But she had been upset by it, because she knew his daughter, and it had been some time before she told Madge. "Don't tell Dad," she said. "He'd tackle him about it. I'll go round the front. Reginald's just sad."

"Of course," she went on, "if he tries anything on Edward ..."

But it appeared that Edward was safe, that Reginald appeared among the garages only when Joan approached. "He only tries it on girls," she said. "It kills Judith though. She knows about it ... and she knows we all know."

"Are you sure it wasn't Reginald?"

"I told you no, Mum."

"We're both upset, I expect," said Madge at last. "It's a bad time of year. Why don't we make some tea?" They set about it.

Madge knew that the comfort she derived from Joan transcended their family relationship: it was an understanding between two women. She was glad of it: the evening with Patrick had, finally, left her tense and angry. She hoped she had not shown it.

Later, in her bed, she found it hard to sleep. Why, she thought, did I not want to go back to the house? Was it to show that it was not just a convenient bed? She now ached with the physical need which she had denied earlier.

Why can't I sort myself out, she thought. Either I do want to go on with it on his terms, or I don't. He had kept away, effortlessly, from their area of disagreement, but he had done more than that. Because nothing he said had been constructive, because he had not talked about the future, he had surely given her a clue to it: this was all there would be. She had wanted a new start; he was satisfied with a resumption.

But she was not certain: she did not know for certain about the other woman. Now she began to ache with the emotional need, which he would not satisfy, for what she must not demand - commitment. Without it, everything they did together was hollow, a structure without a core. By keeping off 'tow-path' talk, as she had promised she would, they were keeping off all that mattered.

At once she put the counter-argument. But *why* is it hollow? We do the same things, he acts the same way, he's just as exciting, just as kind. Why make a fuss about it? Perhaps it's the time of the month. Perhaps next time will be better.

She could hear Martin: he was sleeping badly, and had moved into Robert's room. He doesn't. she thought, even bother to feel sorry for himself. The thought entered her mind - its absurdity taking some time to become obvious to her - that she might ask him for advice. He was thoughtful, sound, and would take it seriously.

Of course he would, she thought. I could, absolutely, rely on it. And yet there was a time when he would sometimes even hit me. She could not quite remember why - only that their quarrels had sometimes mounted to a pitch at which it was the only possible end. Afterwards he had been sorry; she had been sorry that she had goaded him. She had known it: there were some things, she knew, that she must not say. They had both been guilty, both sorry afterwards, and always closer for a time.

How odd, she thought, that both he and Patrick hit me. Do I want them to? Do I make them?

Joan, too, could not sleep. Christ, she thought. I could almost have told her about Bryan tonight!

XIV

"Deirdre wants us to go round for drinks," said Madge. "Tonight! She's sorry about the short notice."

"We'll have to go," said Martin. "I expect she knows we've been to Tom and Marjorie."

It was after dinner: Deirdre's children had gone to bed. "Lovely to see you both," she said. They embraced ritually. "Do come in. I'd like you to meet Charles."

Charles was large and genial; he stood for a moment, then settled again in an armchair. He was smoking a pipe.

Deirdre launched herself at once: it appeared that solicitors were negotiating. Tom, of course, was being bloody and misrepresenting everything.

"You know yourselves I was never like that. I don't know what's got into him. I suppose *she's* behind it."

Charles seemed to be interested in the story. By his genial presence, by fiddling with his pipe, he showed that he was there. But he said almost nothing.

Occasionally, when Deirdre threw out a challenge, he nodded sympathetically.

"After all, I gave him everything. Now he just wants a newer model."

"Do you know," she went on, "I've realised now what was wrong. He never treated me as a *person* at all. Only as a woman. I shouldn't have put up with it. *She* won't. He'll find out a thing or two. Marjorie isn't one to stand for that."

"Do you ... know Marjorie, then?" said Martin.

"*Know* her! I introduced them!" She threw up her eyes, accepting her own stupidity.

Charles rose ponderously. "Shall I serve the drinks, Deirdre?"

"Yes, Charles. Please do."

He went to a sideboard.

"I was telling you about my solicitor. I had another session. He says Tom ought to give me the car."

"But surely," said Madge, "you don't drive a car!"

"That's not the point, Madge. When we bought it, as a matter of fact, I put up the money. It's not as though he needs it for his work. It would make a lot of difference to us."

"What does his solicitor say to that?" said Martin.

"That's just it, Martin. As I said, Tom's being bloody. We'll just have to fight it."

"Charles ..." said Martin, wrenching the conversation away, and uncertain where it would land.

"Charles, are you interested in motoring?"

Charles settled the state of his pipe, and addressed himself to the question.

"You do realise, Martin, that when they talk about British cars, or foreign cars, it's all nonsense! First of all, you can have British cars made in Europe. Or you have cars, made in Britain, but practically all the parts are made in Europe, or even Japan. Or you may think you're buying a British car ... and it turns out that the British firm is American-owned ..."

"So you mean ..."

"Exactly. There's no such thing as a British car. So if you hear someone say you ought to buy British, then all I say is ... take it with a pinch of salt."

"Are you involved in this sort of thing, Charles?"

"Another thing, of course, you don't only have international cartels, fixing prices, and so on, but you have international unions, demanding more money. I tell you, it's real murder. People just don't know what they're up against."

"Charles," said Deirdre. "I'll take Madge into the kitchen. She can help me with the coffee. You two go on with your motoring talk."

"Of course, dear," said Charles. He turned to give Martin his full attention.

"Shall I tell you where it all went wrong?"

In the kitchen, Deirdre lowered her voice.

"What do you think of Charles?"

"He seems very nice," said Madge. "Very sober, and ...

comforting, I'd say."

"You're so right."

"Have you known him long, Deirdre?"

Deirdre did not answer the question. But she seemed to want to impart a confidence. "Do you know what it is about him?"

She looked embarrassed, slightly girlish. It would be an intimate disclosure. "The thing is ... he makes me feel like a *woman!*"

In the lounge, Martin had arrived at the same subject. It had taken a long time.

"We're both very fond of Deirdre," he said.

"I know, Martin. She's told me about you ... how kind you've been."

"Have you known her long, Charles?"

Charles, too, seemed to want to make a disclosure.

"Deirdre," he said, "is a very remarkable woman."

He seemed to be in difficulty with his pipe. Martin gave him time. "Of course she is, Charles."

But it seemed to be all Charles wanted to say. They waited, in silence, for the women to return.

*

Next morning, Madge and Joan were at breakfast. Edward had gone to school.

"How was Deirdre, Mum?"

"I've no idea, Joan. Honestly, I've seen her on her own, Father's seen Tom on his own, and we've seen them both - the two of us. We still don't know anything about it. The only news is that she might have a ... sort of boyfriend."

"Well, so she should. Don't you think so, Mum?"

"I don't know, Joan. We don't know whether she's comforting herself, or whether Charles was always somewhere about. Or even what he is. She didn't say. But she obviously wanted very much to show him to us. Come to think of it, Tom wanted very much to show us Marjorie."

"Of course, Mum. I've told you before. You two ... you're our universal father and mother figures."

"Oddly enough, they *both* seem to need support."

"That's what I mean, Mum."

Martin came in.

"Oh Madge, I forgot to tell you. You left your umbrella in the car. It's been there quite a time. I brought it in."

"Umbrella! What sort of umbrella?"

"I don't know what sort." He went out of the room and came back with the umbrella.

"Isn't that your umbrella?"

"It is a woman's umbrella," said Madge. She turned to Joan. "I think your father must be having an affair with another woman. No, it isn't mine, Martin."

"I don't think that's very funny, Mother."

Martin put the umbrella on a chair. "It must be Kay's," he said. "I sometimes give her a lift to the station." Kay was a colleague.

"Ah well, you could do worse. She's very well preserved."

Joan was irritated and severe. "Oh shut up, Mother. I must go, anyhow. Goodbye, Father." She kissed him: they were both awkward.

Disconnected by Joan's departure, Martin and Madge went on with their breakfast in silence; they now showed no awareness of each other.

Martin rose and went to the sideboard. Being behind Madge, and with the tension broken, he suddenly felt a wish to talk to her. He hated his lie. He stood for some seconds, silently, until she became aware of it. He returned to his chair, and the moment passed: it had passed for both. They resumed their silent breakfast.

"Do you think I'd be seen *dead* with an umbrella like that?" said Madge, suddenly. She spoke with unusual force, and bitterly.

He looked at the umbrella. "I hadn't noticed what kind of umbrella it was. I suppose it's just an ordinary umbrella ..."

"It's vulgar, and tasteless, Martin."

"Well, never mind. It's only someone's umbrella. Let's not have an argument about it."

"Just the sort of thing I'd expect Kay to have," she said, deliberately.

He said nothing.

"I don't suppose you know the difference between good taste and bad taste. I don't suppose you notice that this house is *tastefully* looked after; that we always have fresh flowers; that everything is *clean* ..."

He tried to placate her. "Oh, come on, Madge. Of course I do."

"You don't. You don't," she said, loudly.

Both were silent for a few seconds. Again he tried to placate her. "Look here, old girl. There's nothing to make a fuss about. Shouldn't you take one of your pills, or something?"

"'Take one of my pills'! 'Old girl'!" She shouted the words. He waited for her to stop, exasperated at his clumsiness. But now she wanted to be unreasonable, to have a violent communication with him. Weeping, she went on.

"Why don't *you* take a pill? Why am I the one who has to? Do you tell *her* she ought to take a pill?"

Martin did not know how to intervene; his face was cast down.

"Why don't you take a pill for ... calm superiority?"

She was angry that she had to weep. He spoke again, calmly.

"I can tell you, Madge, I don't think I'm superior, and I'm certainly not calm. And I do have pills, as a matter of fact."

"You *are* calm," she said, shouting again. "I hate it. Why should I be the one shouting ... and crying, and you sit there ..."

Both were quiet. But she had finished.

It had been a moment of communication. "I suppose I *ought* to take one of my pills," she said, finally.

They still sat at the table. He tried to change the subject violently, to drag their conversation to another level, to show that they had other levels.

"I was thinking, Madge, after seeing Deirdre yesterday: each of them accuses the other about money. It's because money is the only thing between them, and it's quantitative. If one has some, the other can't have it."

He saw that she was listening, had decided to put away her anger.

"Anything else, any meanness or generosity shown in other ways, can be argued about, but it can't be proved."

They were quiet.

"Is Kay ... is *Kay* interested in caravans?" she said.

"Kay! I don't know. What a funny question."

Again they were quiet.

"Madge," he said, indicating by his manner that he was being serious, and that he meant well. "Don't you think ... you ought to take something up? I mean, a part-time job, or something. After all, Joan is getting pretty independent. Edward is very ... self-contained. I'm sure it would do you good."

He had spoken encouragingly, kindly.

"I have thought about it, Martin. I've often wondered what I would do. But what could I do?"

"What about something voluntary? Like social work. You'd be good at that."

She turned to face him, surprised.

"Well, you know, you're interested in people ... articulate. And sympathetic. You know, some kind of guidance. What about marriage guidance?"

She saw that he was serious, and did not meet his eye.

"Why not think it over?"

He looked at the clock: it stood at twenty-five past nine.

"I must go, Madge. I'm late. Let's have another talk about it."

When Patrick had been in the habit of ringing her, it had always been at half-past-nine.

He looked out of the window, and she joined him for a moment. "What a *perfect* day!" she said.

She had nowhere to go; she wondered, for a moment, whether he had.

"You don't say much about *your* job, Martin. How is it all going?"

He seemed surprised. "It's all right, Madge. Irritations, of course, as always. It's a bit wearing sometimes. But ... yes, I suppose it's going all right."

"But ... I mean, do you get any fun out of it now?"

He did not quite seem to understand what she meant.

"It's all right, Madge. Nothing to worry about."

He picked up the umbrella. "By the way, I do need the car today."

"I will think about what you said, Martin."

It occurred to her that if she found a job it would make her emotionally less dependent - upon Patrick. But she knew that for women of her age a job - and the seeking of it - could be a further humiliation. It was a familiar part of women's lore: girls and women younger than herself had protected themselves against it; but she was in the wrong generation, and had married early.

She waited, wondering whether the telephone would ring. She pondered, for a moment, on her split and differing loyalties. She could not blame herself for them: indeed, she wondered whether anyone was clearly to blame - whether, on the whole, everyone was not faithful to everyone else.

*

Martin wanted to drive to Croydon: a site, on a short lease, and a caravan, were for sale there. The agent had insisted that it was a 'mobile home'.

Crossing the river, he confronted, briefly, his own marriage. He did not often think about it; he wanted not to think about it. But today Madge had reminded him of the tight-rope on which he walked. It had never occurred to him not to keep secret his relationship with Liz. He had feared discovery because of the effect it would have on his family. But, he thought, in spite of one's presumed - and real - concern for them, one cannot stop; one cannot refuse life when it is offered.

Deception had solidified the barrier forming between himself and Madge. It was as though he had decided that she must be put outside his protective layer. He knew that that had existed for a long time. It moderated pains, hurts and griefs, it gave him courage, and it protected him in his professional life. He suspected that it was the cause of his physical disorder. But he suspected, too, that it moderated joy and delight. Madge at first, before her other girls and women, his children, sometimes music - all had penetrated his protection and delighted him. Professional success had not.

Liz had penetrated it quickly. But for a time they had tortured themselves, and tortured each other. Each in turn would assert that he would not go on: there must be a decision. They must either leave their partners or stop seeing each other. They had made the second decision many times. There had always been a last time, a sacrificial day.

Sometimes it had been he who had abandoned their decision; sometimes he waited for the letter which would show that she had done so. It would have come to his office, marked 'Private'. His secretary would have left the envelope unopened, on top of his other letters of the day. Each time the result had been the reverse of the pretended intention. Because they had been so plainly relieved, the bond between them had been strengthened. Both had noticed the anomaly: it seemed that the professions and actions of lovers were quite unrelated. Each had seemed to know that if one abandoned the decision the other would.

Time had reduced the need for a definitive solution. Martin found that he had entered a sort of second marriage. By good luck the first had remained, more or less, in equilibrium. He knew that many of his colleagues had secret lives: it was a part of men's lore to know it. One had only - as he had said to Liz - to watch in a pub in the early evening to see that it was true of a large part of the human race. There was always an amused sympathy for the defecting male. 'Good for him', one might say.

The site was graceless, surrounded by petrol stations, yards and shops. There were other caravans. Some accident of planning had left them, if not intended, at least legal. It amused him that that was where he and Liz might alight. It was in a desert: it might be an oasis.

Holding the key, he felt a familiar thrill: he was exploring a new house, perhaps a new life. The caravan was bleak but straightforward. Paint, floor-covering and basic furniture, in the style of the newly-married poor who expected that they would not be poor for long, would suffice.

Martin wanted to tell Liz at once about the caravan. He had tried, but failed, to ring her that morning. Now, but more cautiously, he tried again: there was no reply.

Driving back to London, he remembered times they had spent together. Once they had gone back to her house because she had forgotten to bring a lemon for their picnic.

"We can't have sardines without a lemon," she said. She had insisted, this time, on showing him the house. Ironically, she knocked on a bedroom door. "There's the unmarital bed!" It was one of the few occasions on which she had, even by implication, mentioned her husband. She had, she said, forgotten something else: she fetched a towel and they walked back to the forest.

It had surprised Martin to find her to be emotionally so fragile, and physically - as he had told her - such a waif. Her manner, smart and confident, of the senior doctor's wife, did not square with these. Her breasts were small; when his hands found them he was at first disappointed, but then moved, in a new way. For her it was a new experience; her breasts had slowly come to life. She had not known what they were.

"Of course I knew about erogenous zones," she had said, "*technically*, but I didn't quite believe in them." Remembering the first, impulsive, physical gesture which had so moved him, that had been a surprise. Women must be many-layered: they could be awake at one level, but remain closed at another. Formulating the idea, Martin realised that it was true of himself, of everyone, of the whole of life: it was a truism.

He remembered another time: there had been a snatched meeting in a pub near her home; both had wanted more. They went into the forest. It was raining, and cold. Martin brought a rug and a waterproof raincoat from his car. Just like teenagers hiding from parents, he thought: we 'had sex', just as they do.

They had said little. He had expected that it must start a new cycle in their anguished debate. 'We can't go on like this', she might say. But she did not. Next day, when he rang her, she said: "it was lovely last night, Martin."

"I forgot to say," he said, "that you have lovely breasts." He heard, almost saw, the expression on her face. He had learnt her moods - at least their main complexions. Unable to control them, she loved him for it.

At times he had refused to accommodate to them and had been

angry. For weeks they would struggle to keep apart. Then one or other would recognise that their quarrel had been only another expression of their dilemma. Their anger, the sharpening of their attitudes, even their unreasonablenesses, had only made each more human, and more lovable to the other.

Sometimes they had taken a hotel room: they would arrive in the early afternoon, would pay in advance, and not stay the night.

Once she brought a bottle of whisky. With glee she fondled a card: it read 'DO NOT DISTURB'. The luxury of the room, the warm bed, the bath, the infinite private hours ahead delighted them both. At intervals they went out to the small family restaurants in the area, or to the pub. They were near his College: it pleased them to take the risk that Martin might encounter a colleague; if he did he would wave cheerfully.

But he was not used to whisky, and did not know how much he could drink. Rather suddenly he found himself overtaken by it. Expecting to vomit, and uncertain how drunk he was, he lay on a rug in the bathroom. Amused, not at first anxious, she covered him with blankets and lay beside him.

At intervals he rose, to test his legs, or to breathe deeply. The room, the hotel, the world continued to rock until he returned to the safe, flat floor. He imagined, weaving all around him as they must be, the telephone conversations of the important world - the world of government, university, law, money. He wondered how many of the millions of conversations of a day quite annulled each other. Perhaps at that moment someone was saying 'why not Blake?' - or even 'why Blake?'.

As the hours passed, responsibility returned slowly. He began to pace his return to sobriety, to calculate when he might at least pretend to be sober. Liz ordered coffee for them, and ran another bath.

At last, containing himself, he dressed and they left the hotel. Luck favoured them: both reached their homes without accident, and resumed their authentic lives. It had been, though uncomfortable, a memorable evening, and strangely gay.

3

XV

For the children, family holidays had been times of discovery. The habit remained: each thought that the summer was a watershed. This time Joan would make up her mind about Bryan; John would fight through his diffidence and win his prize; Robert would sort himself out. An adventure was promised for Edward: he had joined a youth orchestra, and it was to tour.

For Martin, the university teacher, each summer was the end of a cycle: the new one promised new ideas, new colleagues, new students, the possibility of change, and progress. He pitied friends whose lives were not thus cyclic, who must, he supposed, simply go on and on. And Madge, carried along by family habits, also thought that summer was the end - and the beginning - of the year.

"Who's your new girlfriend, Robert?" said Joan, at lunch. The family were again together.

"Is that the girl you were telling me about, Robert?" said Martin.

"Yes, Dad. Connie."

"When are you going to bring her around?"

"I will, Dad."

"What about Sandy, John? I haven't seen her for a long time."

"Neither have I, Dad, as a matter of fact."

"Oh ...?"

"It doesn't mean anything, Dad ... either way. It's just ..."

"You've no idea, Robert. It's been like a casualty ward, with these two."

"Go on, Mother," said Joan. "It hasn't been like that at all."

"Well, it's all over now, and no bones broken," said Martin.

"Everyone's fingers crossed, it seems," said Robert. John and Joan looked glum.

"Anyhow," Robert went on, "you're not going to sit about waiting for your results, are you? What about holidays? Sailing, Joan?"

"I'm not sure. Probably."

"Going abroad, John."

"I think so. Dad's kindly giving me one more 'sub'."

"Good old Dad."

To go abroad was, of course, a part of the family culture.

"Switzerland?"

"I'm not sure about that."

"Are you looking for a job?"

"I've had interviews. It seems that if I get a good degree I'm employable; if not, not."

"Of course he'll get a good degree," said Martin.

John looked surprised. "*I'm* not sure, Dad." He did not want to talk about it. It was now the least important thing in his life.

"I might be working in a builders' yard. Or not at all. At least I'll have plenty of company."

His fantasy covered a much wider range than he supposed they thought. He might be working in a restaurant, or writing in a garret: it would probably be abroad. The only certainty was that there would be a perfect girl with him.

"Well, Father and I are just going to sit about," said Madge. "I'm looking forward to it. When Edward goes off you'll all be away."

"Mother's right," said Martin. "No conferences, no examining, no research, no writing. Just sit with her, read - Tolstoy perhaps - walk to the park, eat and drink, and sleep. I'm looking forward to it too."

"And no frantic holiday abroad, pushed in at the last minute."

Why doesn't Liz answer the phone, thought Martin. Will I be able to sit with Madge, for days and days, wearing that mask which conceals what I'm thinking, or not thinking.

Won't he see that I'm not the person he thinks I am? thought Madge. How will I see Patrick if Martin's at home? No evening-class alibis now.

Later, Martin and Madge continued to sit together, as though rehearsing their holiday. The garden path was in view; they had often looked out upon it, watching Joan and Steve, or the other children and their friends.

They were surprised to see Alice. As she came closer Madge said, urgently: "something's happened to her." Alice was out of sight for a few seconds as she came to the door. "I think Jim's left her!"

She rose and opened the door for Alice. Seeing her cracked face, Madge embraced her at once.

"Come in, Alice. Only Martin and I are in."

"He's gone," said Alice. Madge brought her into the house.

Martin rose, and seeing Alice, stretched his hand toward her.

"Jim's gone," said Madge.

"He left me a note. He said he was very sorry, but he couldn't take any more." Alice's voice, too, was cracked..

"Oh, Alice," began Madge. "I don't know what to say. I just hoped it wouldn't happen."

"I hoped it wouldn't happen, too," said Martin.

"Nothing about where he was going, or what we'd do about the house, or even ... what I'd live on."

"That's mean of him," said Madge, cautiously.

"I'm sure I will hear from him."

"I'm sure you will," said Martin.

"I don't even know where he is. I just have to sit it out. I believe women in my position usually ring the office, or stand on the pavement outside. I won't be doing any of that. As a matter of fact, I do understand him."

"What do you mean, Alice?" said Martin.

"I understand not being able to take any more, and doing the one thing that would seem to ... let him off the hook. Of course it doesn't really."

She wept quietly.

"I'm sure I mixed a metaphor in there somewhere."

"I won't say I'm sure he'll be back," said Madge, "because I'm not, of course. But don't you think he might?"

"I don't know, Madge. I don't know whether he's decided this is the only solution, for him ... or for us both, perhaps, or just what he said - that he can't take any more."

They continued to talk about it. Alice did not criticise Jim, so Martin and Madge did not.

"If we can do anything, Alice ..." Madge began.

"Of course, Madge. For the present, just be there."

"We will. But Alice, if it's just that he can't ... take it, he might feel differently after a time."

"Of course he might."

When Alice had gone, Martin and Madge talked about her. They had been moved and upset. It relieved them a little that she had come, and that she seemed to want to keep in touch with them.

"How different," said Madge, "... from Deirdre."

"I wonder if I'll hear anything from Jim," said Martin.

*

"Lovely of you to ask us to dinner," said Tom to Martin. They had met in a pub. Tom had suggested it.

"But actually ... we don't really want to get too near Deirdre, just at present ..."

"I quite see that, Tom. Perhaps we could all ..."

"Grand idea, Martin. Let's ..."

Tom took out his pipe, brandishing it. He seemed preoccupied.

"Fact is, I'm really cheesed. Did I tell you I bought a new car?"

"No, I don't think so, Tom."

"*First* day I had it, it wouldn't start. We have to leave it in the road, of course. It's on a slope. So I put Marjorie in the driving seat, and just got it clear of the car in front ... he'd backed in. Far too close."

He stopped, obviously unable to handle calmly the story he had to tell.

"Unfortunately ... Marjorie doesn't drive, actually ... I didn't realise she didn't know what to do. I only wanted to get it clear, then I'd have got in, put it in gear, and started it that way. Anyhow, it ran forward ... I tried to tell her ... but she didn't understand."

He was quiet for a time.

"*Bashed* into a lamp-post! Couldn't have been going more than four miles an hour. Completely ruined the grille, smashed one of the headlights ..."

Martin expressed dismay, and sympathy.

"Do you know how much they said it would cost? *Eighty-six pounds!* It's outrageous."

"Well of course," said Martin, "that sort of thing always is expensive. It's very labour-intensive."

"'Labour-intensive'!" Tom seemed to snort.

"What about your insurance? Is your discount all right?"

"I'm not sure. Could be worse, unfortunately. They're claiming it was being driven by an unlicensed person. Absolute rubbish! It wasn't being driven at all. It's a complete racket. Actually, to make things worse, Marjorie slightly ... bruised herself."

Martin expressed concern.

"Not serious. Just her forehead. But I can tell you, we're both pretty cheesed ... Of course, she's marvellous ... I can't tell you what a relief it is ..."

He stopped.

"That's all that matters, of course. I've always said, how lucky you two were."

He lit his pipe, and drew heavily on it.

"Did I tell you I had to see my solicitor? Of course I'm always seeing him. But this time he said it was urgent. Rang me up. He said Deirdre was putting something over which might be difficult to stop. I had to go over it all again ... and do you know what? Been there about an hour, I suppose. I thought everything was getting straight ... Suddenly he said: 'do you mind if we stop for today?' *He* couldn't take any more. Asked me to come back in a few days. Extraordinary! As though ..."

He stopped, and looked at Martin.

"I suppose it's all on my mind. But I've been doing all the talking. Haven't even asked how you are. How are you, Martin? How are you both?" An expression of concern shone out of Tom's tortured face.

Martin catalogued the uneventful weeks, the small happenings in his family since he and Tom had last met.

"That's how it always is, Tom, as a matter of fact. Fortunately, I suppose."

"You are fortunate, Martin."

They were quiet for some minutes.

"Of course, the car isn't really important. I'll get it sorted out. But you wouldn't believe how ... annoying it was. New car, too."

Tom was quiet again.

"Tell me, Martin, do you play bridge?"

Martin shook his head.

"I've been thinking. I really ought to take something up. Wouldn't mind some sort of craft. Not hangings, of course, or anything like that. Don't want to compete with Marjorie. I thought marquetry, perhaps. Or even bridge, or chess. You know what I mean? You know, sometimes you feel you're not using all your ..."

"That's exactly why I like talking to you, Martin. Always have."

The gin he had drunk had slightly affected Tom's speech: it seemed as though his tongue had grown a little and was hard to manage.

"Don't know what I'd ... You're so understanding, Martin. Take things as they come. Madge too, of course."

They were quiet for a time.

"Martin, do you ... or Madge ... see Deirdre at all?"

"Yes we do sometimes, Tom, as a matter of fact."

"You know about her fancy man then, I suppose."

"Well yes, actually Tom ... we have met Charles."

"Charles!"

Martin said nothing.

"You haven't met Nevill?"

"No, Tom. Only Charles."

Tom seemed gloomy. "Do you know what I'd like," he said. "Some time ... you and I ... to have a real night out. You know ... get really drunk."

※

Because they worked together, Robert and Connie had had the opportunity to become friends, and they had done so. Sometimes they spent nights together. She was undemanding: unlike the others, she seemed to be satisfied with him. For him it had become an experiment: perhaps it would after all be with Connie that he would sort himself out. Meanwhile, he was glad to have an amiable girlfriend: it was even a protection. He wondered whether the kind of equilibrium in which they had seemed to settle was what marriage offered. But he was wary, and uncertain of himself. He feared that their equilibrium must be a temporary one; he suspected that he had a long way to go before he was sorted out. Neither he nor Connie wanted to move to the other's flat.

They were in a Soho pub, surrounded by friends from the theatre and other denizens of the area. Since Sharon's accusation he had become more aware of the presence around him of homosexual men: they were, he saw, quite easy to identify - that part of schoolboy lore was correct. It was, he presumed, because they must proclaim themselves in order to have any identity at all. He saw that he was attractive to them as well as to girls. But, he thought, that doesn't mean I am one. He had tested himself, absorbing the importunate gaze of one after another. It surprised him how boldly they stared as soon as he was alone. If Connie left him for a minute it was as though they hoped to detach him from her before she returned. So he stared too, and, he was convinced, felt only distaste.

He had begun to talk to Connie about the theatre: she was interested in its purposes; he began to formulate and refine his conception of it. His duties were multifarious, but imprecise: he was neither producer nor stage manager, but a little of both.

"Why don't you just produce?" said Connie. "You could. Not necessarily here. Why don't you try to move into that?"

He saw that she was urging him to better himself; memories of his home and youth pressed him toward an adverse reaction. But this was different: if he did, it would be of his own doing. And Connie was of his own tribe, and entitled to an opinion.

"Do you really think so, Connie?"

"Of course I do. Have a go. Make them give you a go."

It could be, he thought, my turning-point. It could be when I take charge of my life. It could even be with her. For a time, anyway.

"Watch my beer, Connie," he said.

In the lavatory he looked at the *graffiti* above him. Obscene drawings, verse and messages covered the wall. Some had been heavily blotted out; others, more recent, or thought by someone to be harmless, remained for the amusement of the customers.

Among them were carefully written, detailed requests for sexual attention. Robert read: 'I'm fifty. I like boys and have a lot to offer. I will be at the corner of Charlotte Street and Mortimer Street at six o'clock tomorrow. I will be wearing a red tie.' The message was signed, and dated a few days earlier.

Robert felt sympathy for the unknown, probably unlovable man in his call for love. One must surely be in the extremities of need to expose oneself - perhaps to danger and humiliation - with such desperation. Or perhaps the need had been for danger and humiliation.

He read another: it was obscene in its phrasing and in the nature of its demands. It concluded: 'I will be in the toilet 1.00 to 1.15. Put a note over the door'. The message was signed with two Christian names - one masculine and one feminine - and dated that day.

Robert looked at his watch: that was the time. Sounds from the single, closed cubicle showed that it was occupied. He was overcome with terror. He hurried out and joined Connie. He grasped her hand. For a time they said nothing: whatever they felt flowed through their joined hands.

"Come to my place tonight?" he said. She moved her head a little, signifying assent.

Surely, he thought, that means I'm not one. He had been slightly reassured by his terror.

*

Slowly, and resisting it, Joan had changed her opinion about Bryan. As lover, and sailor, he had been expert and exciting. On the boat he had talked little; she had basked in love and sun. But since then, when they talked, he had begun to reveal mean opinions. Once he made a remark about Martin which angered her.

"I call that snide. You don't know him. Why should you say that? Why should you say anything about him?"

"Ah, that got into you, didn't it, my kitten!"

"I'm not a kitten, Bryan. Let alone your kitten."

"I'm only saying that he's on to a good thing. I've seen them ...

dropping in to give the odd lecture ..."

"Them! Bryan? You mean professors? Or do you mean miners ... or blacks? Them! If we're going to talk, and not just ..."

"Screw, Joan?"

She swept the remark away with a gesture. "If you're talking about my Dad, I can tell you it's not just the odd lecture. He works twice as hard as you, as a matter of fact."

A new expression appeared on his face: she saw a cowardly look.

"Let's forget it," she said.

As she walked home she felt anger and sadness, but also the beginnings of a release. Taking the short cut through the garage she started to run, longing for the solitude of her room. As she rounded the last corner she heard someone behind her.

She stopped and turned: it was Reginald. But this time she would not try to escape him. Uncertain what she would do if he came nearer she stood, facing him. I'll say: 'Ah, the Kensington rapist', she thought. Or I'll just kick him in the balls.

He stopped: she saw that this time he had not meant to molest her. They separated, awkwardly. He seemed to want to ask me something, she thought.

She had seen, on Reginald's face, the expression, not of cowardice, but of defeat. She felt unexpectedly sorry for him.

Suddenly she wanted the young, immature, uncomplicated hesitations of Steve: she would ring him later.

XVI

John was travelling to France. He was sure the journey would be fateful for him. On the ship, surrounded again by the young and beautiful, he wrote in his diary.

Monday - on the ship
I've decided to keep a diary again. I must honestly analyse my motives. Then if I fail, at least I'll know why.

There's a sort of happiness in the act of travelling - quite different from arriving. It's like the frog again: he sees what's moving. I seem to be satisfied only when I'm moving. I can understand what it must be like to be a gypsy. I love ships and trains, and stations at night when they're full of sleeping travellers - all wanting to go somewhere next day - and *pensions*, when I stay just a few days. Not 'planes, though, even if I could afford them. And I love the excitement of *Postes Restantes* - where one might pick up the letter which will say where she is! I'm sure I've seen that happen. At Marseilles, perhaps, telling one to go to Aix. Of course I've only picked up exam results.

She! Why do I think I'll find her abroad? It's because I'm rejecting the deceptions of propinquity, and I want to make the gesture of rejecting them. I'm not looking for the girl in the tennis club, or the girl next door. I don't want even the preconceptions of propinquity. I want the sudden recognition of perfection - wherever it may be. That's what I saw in the Swiss girl. I've learnt something from that. I won't moon about next time!

Of course in some ways it must be harder while travelling. Perhaps she'll be travelling as well, with the same motives. Then our paths may cross only for a day. I may recognise her at once, but will she recognise me?

I honestly think *I'll* know at once. Surely that particular kind of look, that complete sympathy, shining out of a pair of eyes, conveys more than a lifetime of words.

I know it's not so simple. A woman is a body, as well as eyes. Every man has formed his philosophy of a woman's body - he has watched so many. If the eyes alone aren't enough, what about the eyes and the body? Surely they must be enough! I know that character, intelligence, sensuality, may not *necessarily* be mirrored by them, but I don't want to live in that world. I must deny it, or at least ignore it.

If I meet her, and recognise her, I must throw off my shyness and act at once. What if she doesn't respond at all, or responds *too* eagerly. I mustn't draw back. I know how easy it is to pretend that it's the other's fault - to protect oneself against the humiliation of failure. I must press forward, must expose myself honestly and purely. A life - two lives - may depend on it.

Why am I writing all this? What will I think if I read it in a year's time? Is writing a smoke-screen, a substitute for action? I must make sure it isn't.

Wednesday - Dieppe

It's strange how contented I feel here. I ought sometimes to be bored, or lonely, but I'm not. I'm only just abroad - just about the nearest point to England. But I'm quite disconnected from it. When I go back - *if* I go back, I'll have to look for a job. I don't want to think about that at all.

I like this town. It's strangely unaffected by the tourists on their way to Paris. They don't even get out of the train! I like its Frenchness, and I hate the American paperbacks in the bookshops which try to deny it. I don't talk to English speakers, British or American, because I want to be in France. My awful French just gets me along.

I know I can hardly hold a serious conversation in French with anyone. If I met her I'd have to speak in English; perhaps she'd speak in French. Am I deliberately looking for her? I think that just below the conscious boundary of my mind I'm expecting the encounter. By writing in this diary I'm preparing for it.

I like best sitting in the cafés, where I can write this, or just watch, listen and think. I like especially the small cafés run by families, when the family itself spends its evenings there. I enjoy the good humour and warmth - and the activity. Do foreigners live more warmly among their families than we do, or is it that I don't quite understand what is being said, and trivialities seem more than trivial? I used to wonder about this in Switzerland.

Is it that the detached position I occupy exactly suits me? Perhaps I have a wish for warmth but don't want to get too close to it. Do I write this to make it unnecessary to talk to people? Anyhow, I dine in one of the cafés, then stay - if there is a part of the café which allows it - for another hour or two. I know it can't go on for ever, but I love it.

What do I think about? I know I'm too introspective and analytical, always working out a theory of my own life. Oddly enough, I don't expect to find her among the café families. I think I expect to find her in a *pension*. Ideally, I would like to stay in a family hotel with its own café. Then she, like myself, would spend hours in the café. But why should I expect any particular kind of encounter? Surely its whole essence must lie in unexpectedness - in lack of calculation. As a matter of fact, my *pension* is really very seedy. I have a weakness for seediness, fortunately, because it's all I can afford. Do I expect her to have the same weakness?

I think I might move tomorrow.

Thursday

Last night I went up to my room earlier than usual. It's not often that I'm willing to waste evening hours in sleep, but I was tired after walking, and expecting it would be my last night here.

I didn't want to separate myself entirely from the town, so I opened the shutters in my room. Outside it was clearly a back street, but hard to place. I've noticed before how quickly French towns descend into seediness, and recover again, almost within yards. There was no-one in the street.

I couldn't help focusing my attention on a room almost opposite. It was very dimly lit and a grille on its window hindered my view, but I could see that a woman was sitting there, quite near the window. She seemed to be busy, but she looked up often from whatever she was doing. I wasn't sure whether she could see me. I hadn't turned on the light in my room and now I didn't. I looked for a long time; she just carried on and at last I closed my window and went to bed.

I lay awake for some time. Had she seen me? Or rather, had she noticed me? I was very conscious of the barriers - the walls and windows, and the street - between us. I expect the real barriers are much more formidable. But I have decided to stay another day.

This morning I couldn't see anything. The day was bright but the room opposite was dark. I've thought about her at times through the day, curiously rather than obsessively. I suppose it was inevitable that I would want to see if she was there this evening. I've been up to my room several times, but there's no light in hers. I'm writing this in a café, and wondering if I will see her again.

Friday

When I finally went back to my room last night I did see her. It was dark, and there was no light in her room, but this time her window was open. I could easily have thrown an apple - or a flower - into her lap.

Nothing could have been simpler or more straightforward. She seemed to be looking directly across toward me. Had she seen me the night before? Perhaps she had noticed me in the streets and identified me as the one she'd seen.

At least she wasn't with anyone, or if she was, she had chosen to detach herself. I felt sure that she had given me an opportunity to act - a coded invitation.

I wondered whether to try to speak in French, but decided that, though courteous, it would be ridiculous. In English I could at least say exactly what I wanted to say: she would surely see the point of that. She might even be fluent in English herself.

Her hands were out of sight but again she seemed to be busy - perhaps sewing, or embroidering. But she didn't look down: she simply looked, steadily, and smiling a little. She seemed to be dark, rather than fair, but I couldn't be sure. I've always known how I can be captured by a direct gaze. It's ironic that this time I could hardly see her eyes.

Anyway, I didn't hesitate, but said, as clearly as I could, though quietly, and trying to project my voice across the street: "I must tell you that I saw you last night. But you've opened your window tonight."

She didn't say anything, but just gazed, and continued to smile.
"I don't know who you are. But may we meet?"
She still didn't say anything.
"I'm sure it will be important. For me, at least."

I was rather carried away, told her my name, and said: "may we meet tomorrow morning, and walk on the beach? May we meet at ten?"

Again she didn't answer. She seemed to gather together whatever she'd been working on, and very slowly and quietly got up and moved back, disappearing into the room behind.

I waited for some time, wondering what to do. I did not think I could have offended her by the directness of my approach. Was I being tested? I watched hopefully for a sign. After a time I closed my window and went to bed - but not to sleep. It had seemed to me that my fate was to be decided within seconds: those seconds were stretched over a night.

I can't criticise her. There can be many reasons for her silence: perhaps I'll find out what they were. I thought last night that my direct approach was the only pure one, and I still think so.

What is a night's wait in a lifetime? My mind tossed and turned; I know that I fell asleep only because I know that I woke up. In a second my mind was filled with the same thoughts. It was not yet light, and I was impatient.

This morning I saw that her window was closed: I hadn't heard it being done. I decided I could only act as though she had heard - and understood - my invitation. I thought she might be waiting outside my *pension*, at ten o'clock; or perhaps she would have gone to the beach. So I walked to the beach at half-past-nine, and returned by the only road she could have used. I couldn't be sure which building she lived in because only its back faced mine. It seems to be some kind of apartment. I can hardly penetrate one of them and ask for her. How could I describe her? So I spent a few hours waiting in the street, hoping that she'd come out of one of the doors. By eleven o'clock I knew that my invitation had failed.

I've spent the rest of the day walking around the town, from her street to the beach, the market place, the cafés, and the docks. I like the life and bustle of the market - even though I know I won't buy anything. Most of the stall-holders seem to be from the town, but some are Arabs, or Tunisians. I suppose it's the same thing that sends me to the cafés - a sort of wish to immerse myself a little in what seems to be the life of the people. But I'm sure I haven't seen her anywhere. Of course, I hardly know what she looks like! I've decided, if I don't see her tonight, I'll definitely move on tomorrow.

Saturday
Last night she wasn't there. I couldn't bear to spend the evening in my room. I'm sure it worried Madam to see how often I went in and out of the *pension*. I was annoyed at my failure, of course. But I'm disappointed in her: I think she has failed too. I've decided to stay one more night.

Sunday
I stayed late in the cafés. I think I was unwilling to be reminded of my failure by seeing her closed window. When I went back to my room, again she wasn't there.

I got up early to have breakfast in one of the cafés. This time the window was open but she wasn't there. I walked around the town once more and went back to my room to pick up my haversack. Of course I looked across the street toward the window opposite. There was only an old Arab woman sweeping, or perhaps arranging something on the floor.

*

Edward had been lucky to join the youth orchestra. His assumption that he would always pass tests when it was necessary to do so had been shaken. But through the defection of others he had scraped his way in. Now he was the second oboe of two. The first oboe was a girl of his own age, fresh-faced, a little awkward, not quite sure how to handle her new body.

As the orchestra rehearsed before its tour she took control of Edward. She was a good player: when he floundered she knew it and helped him. Sometimes she exaggerated the rhythm by her movements; when he was lost she whispered the bar numbers.

When his own part was exposed she listened attentively and when he did not disgrace himself she nodded her approval.

At first the orchestra was disjointed and incoherent. Slowly the conductor brought it together: the players began to feel themselves to be an orchestra, to listen to each other.

Once he stopped them suddenly. "I knew you'd do that," he said. "You ran away. You panicked because it was difficult. Remember, have courage, but *relax*!" It was an important lesson.

Edward began to enjoy the rehearsals, to be sorry when they were over. He did not know whether it was the same for the others. Most of the players were older than he was and the habits of school made him shy in their company.

But he and Margaret talked together. It was the first time he had been in relationship with a girl of his own age.

"You'll play even better when you get to know each other," said the conductor one day. It turned out to be true. When they began their tour, travelling in coaches, sleeping in hostels, boys and girls began to form pairs. It helped the orchestra to cohere: the discipline of their playing was better because of the new glue.

Edward knew that this was very different from his school quintet. Then the main concern had been to get safely through. Now there was a reality, some representation of what the composer had intended. Because he was surrounded by players better than himself, he began to feel, at last, that he was a part of the music of which he had already been passionately aware. He became more and more involved: it was the best thing that had happened to him.

He had seemed to get through the concerts without disgrace; his place in the orchestra was safe. He was delighted that he had had a modest success in something for which he knew he had little talent - in the ordinary, real world, not in the refined world of his imagination. He had begun to realise that there was a refined world in the interpretation of music: remarks by the conductor had sometimes pointed to it.

The orchestra worked hard: they rehearsed, performed, travelled, and slept, with no time for anything else. The sense of unanimous purpose added to the intensity of Edward's experience, to the depth of his involvement. It could go on for years - perhaps five or six! The future stretched before him with a new promise: there was no reason why it should not be full of delights and excitements.

The last concert was in London. Before it Margaret took Edward's oboe. "I thought there was something wrong with it," she said. She opened her case and brought out sticking plaster and a pair of scissors.

"This will keep you going until you can get it done properly." She worked at it for some minutes.

"It happens to mine sometimes." Edward felt again, as he had felt several times in the days before, a new and indefinable sensation. He knew it was a love feeling: it seemed to encompass, lightly, both his mind and body. It was quite different from his first experience of sexual feeling. That had happened while rope-climbing at school, had been quite clearly localised in his genitals, had not been even obviously pleasurable. He had known at once that the sensation - like the instinctive clutching of newly born babies - came from his deep ancestry, and he had been amazed by it. Now, while his body prepared, quite punctually, he wondered how, and when, the two would be reconciled. He began to see why everyone talked about them.

Walking home, carrying his oboe in its case, his thoughts hovered around the happenings of the weeks before. He was full of hope, and the beginnings of new understandings.

A group of youths watched him. Their posture proclaimed that they were part of the detritus of a rearranged society; the children of his family would have felt sympathy - and some alignment - with them; the parents would have felt sympathy and fear. They were not conspicuous, as black youths would have been; their dress announced, not that they were ominous, but that they belonged to an ominous generation.

"What's he got?" said one.

"It's a clarinet," said another.

They looked at each other and around at the street. It was not yet dark and there were people about.

As he passed them, Edward felt their detachment and contempt.

To have to pass through danger was common: the world was an extension of the playground and he had learnt how to deal with it there. Inferior force, deployed bravely and angrily, often intimidated the enemy.

Undetermined, and desultory, the youths gathered themselves and followed him slowly.

XVII

Madge had taken the train to Brighton and was attending to her house; Patrick would come later. It had been hard to lay an alibi and she was ashamed of it. It had tripped her into dissatisfactions.

Her idea, inexact but bold, that the house would give her an independence, had been compromised. She had handed it to Patrick; he had been merely amused, pleased at the practicality of it. It's not my house now, she thought. It's a convenient bed.

She feared that her affair with him was static, and so must decay. She had held to her promise, and had not asked about the other woman. She wondered if she could bear, again, to go through the ordeal of a break. She had tried not to show her resentments.

And all the time, she thought, it slowly flows away. You begin to fear it, you think you notice the signs, eventually you can't ignore them. You press all the buttons you can, but finally, nothing happens: it's just switched off.

Leaning on the promenade rail, she looked toward the sea, over the beach. It's all there, she thought: children, the unsatisfied young, paired-off couples, young families, the inelegant middle-aged, and the slow elderly. She was not quite sure whether she fitted. She had not bathed for years. She and Martin had joined their swimming children at first, but the sea had grown colder each year.

She felt, suddenly, hands on her waist. She did not turn.

"How gorgeous!" she said.

"I got away early," he said. "Quick. I'm on the yellow lines." They ran to his car.

The exciting, sudden beginning delighted her. It's going to be all right, she thought, and we've got hours.

"Why don't we swim?" she said.

"Of course! Have you got a costume?"

"No, but I've got towels." They drove to the house then, arm-in-arm, walked back to the shops to buy costumes. It's a new thing, she thought. We've never bathed together, or even bought anything together. We never walked arm-in-arm in London.

On the beach he said suddenly: "Look at him!" A middle-aged man walked slowly toward the sea; he wore an old-fashioned swimming costume covering his chest. He left his shoes at the water's edge. They watched as he moved cautiously into the water, measuring the temperature at each step. He seemed to be performing a duty, not enjoying a pleasure.

"That's the worst possible way of doing it."

"Of course," she said. "I quite agree."

They joined hands, ran down the beach and into the water, immersing themselves at once, defeating the cold.

She loved the new thing they had done. She loved his lack of hesitation, and his physical naturalness. "You're a good swimmer, aren't you," she said. He fitted, perfectly, a particular male image - a man in swimming trunks - and he swam the crawl stroke strongly. Unexpectedly she was shy, showing him for the first time a particular female image. She swam the breast stroke, reliably and slowly, her head above the water.

How little we really know about each other, she thought.

"We'll keep your swimming things down here," she said. "I never thought I'd go in bathing again."

I *could* have two lives, she thought. They lay, hand in hand, on the pebbles, uncomfortably, and only just above the threshold of coldness. In a few weeks it would be warmer. Surely, she thought, I could think of some arrangement.

"I liked that," he said. "And only two hours ago I was taking a class."

"Come on, Patrick. I'm bad-tempered if I get cold."

They walked back to the house. "Doesn't it make you feel gorgeous!" she said. "There's nothing like it."

She prepared a supper for them. "Would you open the wine? And have a go at this. I can never do them." She handed him a tin of anchovies. He fitted the key to the flap expertly, starting again, dismissing her attempt. She watched: it came off cleanly.

"That makes me think of Penny," she said. "She asked her husband to look up a train in a timetable. 'I can never understand them', she said. Hubby went off, and of course, we could see he was doing it. 'Somewhere in there lies the secret of happiness', she said."

"Does it, Madge?"

"One of the secrets. There's a kind of harmony if he's seen to be doing the male things, and she the female things. Seen by both. I'm sure it's good for them."

She steered him to the arm-chair. "Do your male thing. Read the paper while I lay the table."

"It's better than pebbles," he said. They lay on the bed: she held him tightly.

"But I *loved* going in swimming. That was quite momentous, as a matter of fact."

"It's to do with skin." He stroked her skin, gently.

She wanted to talk.

"I think I must just love first times. First time in bed, first picnic, first time in my bed, first time swimming together ... Let's have some more. Fix something up, Patrick, will you, please?"

"Of course I will, Madge."

"I love places too. Here, the Downs, now the sea, all the ... discreet places in London we went to - the pubs, even old towpath at times. And your flat, of course."

"And all those other first times," she went on. "Like you pulling the sheet away, secretly touching me, making me put my hand on your leg in the car ..."

She was moved by her own declarations; her face pressed into his shoulder. "Every teenager must have her list, and here am I, practically a grandmother - or at least I could be - going through it all again. And I love your smell!"

"Well, that's good. What a relief! We had dire warnings at school about that."

"I love it. Not after-shave, or hair-cream, but good honest you. And your pectorals. Now I've seen you swimming I know how you got them."

"That was gym. I must say ... they never mentioned *why* we had to get fit."

"Anyhow ..." she began.

He waited. "Yes ...?"

"What about me? I mean how do *I* look in my swimming costume? That was a first time too."

"Why, Madge, how you always look, of course. Trim."

She was quiet for a time. "Are you sure you don't mean 'ship-shape'?"

"No, Madge. Trim."

"Well, I suppose many women would be grateful for that ..."

"I've always been grateful for it."

It was the first compliment he had paid her that day. She tightened her hold, pretending to stop him.

Both had fallen asleep. Waking in the narrow bed, she found his weight, which at other times she loved, uncomfortably upon her. She extricated herself and lay alone, unwilling to wake him.

It had taken her some moments to understand where she was, and guilts had swept through her. She had often had a moment of overwhelming shame, finding herself in the wrong bed, with the wrong body beside her.

It was also the wrong house. Now, unexpectedly, she felt ashamed that she had bought her house without telling Martin. It was, surely, a trivial offence by comparison with the other, but it was a meanness. A new thought had entered her mind: was it possible that Martin had deliberately blinded himself to her doings, or, perhaps, pretended to blind himself. And, if so, had he done it for her, or for himself - for a quiet life?

Patrick, now awake, looked at her curiously.

"*Post coitum ...?*" he said.

"No, Patrick. Just guilts. I always get them when it's been particularly gorgeous ... and all today has been. Swimming ... and love. I'm sorry it's my only adjective today."

"Cheer up, Madge. We're not the first, or the last. I *do* know about it, believe it or not."

"Not now, surely, Patrick!"

"Always, Madge."

They were quiet, holding each other uncomfortably.

"It's like the doubts - and panic - you have in the middle of the night," she said. "But with something really to panic about. It didn't happen so much at first. I think I wanted to punish Martin for not being perfect. But why should he have to be perfect?"

"Why, indeed!"

"It's worse today because I had to lie to Joan."

"I was sorry about Martin too, Madge. I knew him, and liked him. What had he done to me? Of course, I haven't seen him for a long time."

"That's a pity, too, Patrick."

She wanted to change the subject.

"This bed's too narrow," she said.

"One goes in ascending waves," he said, "... of involvement. No doubts, and impossible to stop, committing oneself, then suddenly ... Wham! Back to what one should have first thought of; what everyone else thinks at once."

The word, the mention of commitment, excited her. To me?

"Yes, Patrick, let's cheer up."

She could feel his arm, around her neck, tightening a little. "You're looking at your watch," she said. "That's rude!"

He laughed. "What time shall I get you back?"

"Ten o'clock, if you can manage it."

"We'd better start shifting then." Neither seemed anxious to be the first to move.

"Can we go to your flat, next time?" she said, suddenly.

She felt, again, a slight tension in his arm.

"It's one of our places, Patrick. I loved our times there."

She detached herself and knelt on the bed, her back against the wall. Deliberately, she covered herself with the sheet.

"Why can't we go to your flat?"

He said nothing. She stared angrily, and suddenly shouted her realisation.

"You needn't tell me. *She's* there!"

She knew it to be true.

"Well, isn't she?" She swore at him, dragging out words she had not used for years. "Isn't she? She's there, isn't she! She's living with you."

"Yes, she is, Madge."

She jumped off the bed and began to pick up her clothes, scattered on the floor.

"What's ... this, then?" She pointed to the bed. "Just an extra? Something for Thursdays?" She shouted the phrases.

"Does *she* know about it?"

Weeping, and clumsy, she tried to put on her clothes, now angry that she was being seen naked. Grotesquely half-dressed, she picked up a bundle of his clothes and threw them at him.

"Get out of my bed! Get out of my house!" She swore at him again.

Unable to speak, she went out of the bedroom, carrying her clothes. He got out of bed and dressed. Downstairs, in the sitting-room, he found her sitting, remote, not now weeping.

"It's time we went," he said.

"I'm just waiting for you to go," she said, utterly cold. "I'm not coming with you."

"Don't be silly, Madge! Let me take you back."

"Silly!" Her anger rose again. "I'm never coming with you again. I'm never going to see you again."

As she said it she knew, at last, that it was true. In the past she had changed decisions over minutes: what had seemed to be ends had turned into beginnings. But this was the end. All the joys, the subtleties, the harmonies of their affair would be written off and buried in the anger of a stupid scene. It was what she wanted. She hated him, and that would make it easier.

He was angry too: he spoke coldly and forcefully. "Before you start swearing at me again, just remember what happened. You rang me, you asked me to come here. 'No tow-path talk' you said. What did you expect?"

"Expect! Not just something for Thursdays!" She went around the room, trying to throw things at him.

"What does *she* expect?"

"Stop it!" He caught her arms but she twisted herself away and ran out to the kitchen.

"Slut! Bitch!" He followed her around the kitchen; she tried to hit him with plates. Her anger became wilder: she threw anything she could grasp. Broken crockery and food began to litter the floor.

"Go on. *Hit* me! Hit me again." She saw him clench his fist. "*Mugger!*"

He withdrew his interest, suddenly, and went out to his car. In the street one or two neighbours watched anxiously.

She went to the window and opened it. "Is she better in bed?" she shouted. The neighbours said nothing; one went indoors to fetch her husband.

He got out of the car and came to the window.

"I'll tell you one thing," he said, quietly, and deliberately: she knew it would be cruel.

"She's no *passenger!*"

She was too shocked to reply. He drove away quickly. She closed the window and threw herself on the floor, moaning and weeping quietly. The neighbours went back to their houses.

She lay for a long time, unable to gather herself for the journey home; it was so late that she must leave the house as it was. Perhaps she would leave that for ever too.

At the station, two policemen watched her curiously. They saw the wildness of her manner, but they saw that she was expensively dressed.

"Leave it alone," one said to the other. "If she's got a ticket, and gets on the train." If there was trouble, it would be for the guard, or the police at Victoria.

In the train her fellow-passengers were embarrassed, but finally, relieved. She did not try to hide her angry despair.

"I'm terribly late, Joan. I'm sorry."

"Don't worry about that, Mum. I can look after myself."

"What's the matter, Mum?" Her mother's face had come under the light.

"Are you all right, Mum?"

Madge could not answer.

"Did something happen on the train?" Joan put her arm around Madge and held her tightly.

Madge nodded: she knew Joan would not ask about it.

"Are you all right now?"

Madge nodded again. "I'm so tired."

"Go to bed, Mum. I'll make you a cup of tea. I'll bring it up." They walked slowly towards the stairs.

"Here's your tea, Mum." Joan sat on the edge of the bed.

"Mum ... don't think about it now if you don't want to. But would you mind ... you and Dad ... if I went sailing with Steve next time? Not with the usual crowd."

"Steve! I didn't know he sailed."

"He doesn't, Mum. But we've talked about it, and he'd like to. I'm sure I could teach him."

Madge was glad to be distracted.

"I won't think about it now, Joan. I'll talk to Dad."

"Thanks, Mum."

"Steve! I'd never have thought of him as an outdoor type. I think of him more as a ... studious sort of boy."

Joan concealed a slight irritation as she arranged the sheets and blankets around her mother: it was the ritual of tucking in a slightly annoying child, now performed in reverse.

"There's another thing, Mum. Afterwards, will you mind if Brenda stays with us for a time?"

"Of course not, Joan. Why ...?"

"She can't bear it at home just now. Her parents are splitting up, probably. I said I was sure you wouldn't mind."

"Oh dear! Poor Brenda. Of course she can come. As long as she likes."

"I knew you'd say that. You won't have to entertain her. But you ... and Dad, you're so calm and safe. It'll be nice for her."

They kissed. Madge knew she would be asleep in minutes. She was glad Martin had not yet come home and would not see her.

XVIII

Next morning Madge knew, as soon as she awoke, that sadness would again be with her for a long time. She remembered what she had said to Alice: it had been as though a great hole had been cut in her. She would go to see Alice: a visit would be, she was sure, an exchange of woes, but perhaps comforting for both.

Outside Alice's house she noticed small signs of disarray. She was a little relieved when Alice came to the door.

"Come in, Madge. It's nice to see you." Alice wore an artist's smock. Brushes, carelessly put down, and tins of paint, lay about.

"Take no notice!" But it was impossible not to notice: the house had become an artist's studio; it would be turned into a painting. In the hall a fearsome mural began; it spread erratically into other rooms. "I know what you'll say."

Madge did not know what to say. Bland interest would be absurd; to say what she thought would be cruel - she feared for her friend's sanity. She delayed her answer by following the image from one room to another. She saw that Alice had used the great crack, had embellished and multiplied it, had let loose an orgy of cracks.

"You think I'm off my nut, don't you."

"I don't think that, Alice."

"We all are, as a matter of fact. The ... arrogance of thinking your *doodles* are significant."

"It's alarming, of course. You mean it to be, don't you."

"I mean it to be *obscene*, Madge."

Madge saw that it was true.

"I know all about the paintings of the insane, Madge. They aren't like this at all." Alice seemed tired but obsessive. Madge wondered how to bring her back, for a time at least, to the ordinary world, where husbands walked out and friends made cups of tea.

"Well, to put it at its lowest, Alice, you can't sell it." Madge grimaced at the tactlessness of her remark. That, they had assumed, had been the problem from the beginning.

"Shall I make us some tea?"

"Yes, Madge. That would be nice." Madge saw that Alice was

impatient. She had removed herself into the world of illusion and dreams, of the artistic principle. Was there not a story about an artist who went *into* his painting and disappeared? It was what she had done. She would not want to talk about Jim, about arrangements to be made, or about the future. Madge would make her visit short.

"I think it's exciting, Alice," she said, insincerely. "I'll come again in a day or two: see how you're getting on."

"Yes, do," said Alice. For a moment she seemed to look back into Madge's world.

"We're worried about you, Martin and I, of course. Don't forget."

"I know, Madge. But really, I'm quite O.K." She seemed to realise that she had been perfunctory. "Of course I'm glad you came. I'm glad to see you."

"Don't you want to talk about anything, Alice? Have you seen Jim?"

"Don't you see, Madge: his going has given me new insights, and *that's* the important thing."

"Insights! Into what, Alice?"

"Into myself." She seemed puzzled at Madge's puzzlement. "Don't you realise, this is the best thing that's ever happened to me!"

Madge did indeed think that her friend was going off her nut. There would be no-one to watch her, to see that she came to no harm. A real burden was to be shouldered, real dangers and anxieties were to be faced. She could not look forward to it. She badly wanted to talk to Martin. She had forgotten, for the time being, her own sadness. She saw that in Alice's inward world that would no longer count, perhaps no longer exist.

She had observed before how friends would cluster around one of their number in mental distress. Love and devotion would be offered, but no-one had been certain whether what he had done had not been exactly wrong. It was suspected that even doctors and psychiatrists did not know what to do: how should loving friends!

*

"Who are all those women?" said Jim to Martin, on the phone. "I must have spoken to three or four before I got through to you."

"I'm glad you've rung, Jim."

"Come and have a drink, Martin? Usual place, opening time."

"Of course I will. I'd like to see you."

At the pub, waiting for Jim, Martin wondered what to expect. It would be, he was sure, quite different from the harangue he might have expected from Tom.

With Jim was a young girl. She can't be more than eighteen or nineteen, Martin thought. Hardly older than Joan.

"This is Sophie," said Jim. "This is Martin. I've told you about him."

In her hands a tiny kitten wriggled. "He's an orphan," she said. "He's not weaned yet. I have to feed him every two hours." She seemed to press the kitten to her breast, as though that was where it would be fed. Martin knew, without seeing, that Jim was looking at him anxiously. He was not sure what to say, how much to show he knew. But Sophie seemed not to be anxious.

"I don't know anything about kittens," he said. "Of course, we've had them. But the children always saw to them."

She held the kitten to her face, moaning softly, stroking her cheek with its fur.

Jim went to fetch drinks, leaving them together. Martin still did not know what to say to her. "Whose kitten is it, Sophie?"

"It's my boyfriend's sister's." It was a problematic answer.

"What does your boyfriend do?"

"Oh him! He doesn't do anything. Didn't Jim tell you. He beat me up. I had to go to the doctor."

She seemed so young, Martin thought, even innocent, perhaps vulnerable. But she was curiously absent. Her eyes seemed not to see him; her perfect body seemed disembodied. She could have been, in another era, a witch. He saw that Jim was besotted. Another burden had been placed upon his fragile shoulders. Martin hoped there was some compensation for it.

"You work in Jim's office, don't you, Sophie? What do you do?"

"Continuity mostly. It's very boring, but I don't mind."

Jim returned with drinks. "Hold him for a minute," she said.

Martin and Jim were left together. Martin knew that he must not hesitate. Jim seemed to beg him to speak.

"She's lovely, Jim."

Jim seemed grateful.

"Jim, there's one thing. You asked me not to tell Madge. Does this stand? If I say I've seen you she'll want to know more."

"If you don't mind, Martin, for the time being, let it stand."

Martin saw that argument would be another burden.

"I have spoken to Alice, Martin. I've arranged to see her."

"I'm glad to hear that, Jim. We're worried - about you both - of course."

The kitten was uncomfortable in Jim's hands. When Sophie returned she reached to take it. Every pose of her body, every expression of her face, Martin saw, was perfect. It was an animal perfection: she was the female principle incarnate, the paradigm. But eventually, he was sure, she would absently turn aside, to the boyfriend or another and Jim would be destroyed.

He wished that he could have spoken to Jim alone. He could have said: 'I know she's lovely, Jim. But she'll destroy you. I won't say 'don't'. I'd probably do the same'.

Jim could have said: 'I know I'm a fool, Martin, and I know it won't last. But I can't stop'.

Why, Martin thought, couldn't I have said: 'researching a new play, Jim?' On any other subject they could have teased each other.

As they talked, about office matters, about the kitten, Martin watched Sophie. The sensuality she projected reminded him: a beautiful girl wearing a fur coat made every man who saw her want to be inside it; every man who saw Sophie would be turned into a kitten. No-one could be immune to her - not a judge, or a vice-chancellor, no-one with an ounce of male principle, or a daughter. But to take her on, to connect with that dangerous generation, that was foolhardy. It was Jim, the experienced one, who was vulnerable.

When the two had gone, Martin wondered whether what he and Jim had not said to each other had been implicit. By showing him Sophie, Jim had explained himself; by his manner toward her

Martin had shown that he understood. Both had indicated that Alice was not to be forgotten. He did not think that Jim would want him to meet Sophie again: there was no more to be learnt about her. It might be a long story: it would almost certainly reduce their friendship.

XIX

"I had a drink with Jim," said Martin.

He and Madge again sat, one on each side of their bay window.

"I could see he was full of guilts. He said he'd rung Alice and was going to see her. I told him I was glad."

"Isn't it funny how they all ring each other. Tom rings Deirdre, Jim rings Alice."

"It's safer than actually going to see someone. You can always ring off."

"Well, I went to see Alice. She was very strange, and her painting was ... well, absolutely mad."

She went on to describe her visit. She saw Martin listening intently, preparing to take his share of the burden. She felt, quite unexpectedly, a small surge of love for him.

"I had a shock yesterday," said Martin. "You know those Hare Krishna people - they wear saffron robes and shave their heads - who stop you in the street and try to sell you books. One of them stopped me in the Strand. He had a girl with him. She didn't seem to recognise me, but I'm sure it was Judith."

"Judith! Reginald's Judith!"

"I haven't seen her around for some time. She must have left home; he'll be on his own."

"Poor old Reginald. He does seem to be having a bad time."

"Everyone does, as a matter of fact, Madge."

"Did I tell you Deirdre rang?" said Madge. "She said she wanted some advice. She's coming to see me."

"It'll be what to do about Charles ... and Nevill."

"I can't say anything about that!"

"I don't expect you'll have to, Madge. She'll just talk at you and go away and do whatever she wants to."

"Keep them both, I expect."

"What shall we say to Joan?" said Madge later.

Martin thought for a moment.

"We can only say 'yes', Madge. It's really not our business any more."

She seemed unwilling to agree that the answer must be quite so obvious. Ought they not to struggle a little, and to show Joan that they were struggling?

"I agree, Martin, that's she's quite able to look after herself ... and it's not our business."

But, she thought, do I want her to grow up just yet? But, he thought, what do we mean when we say she can look after herself? He did not want to ask.

They were silent for several minutes.

"Does Steve know how to sail, Madge?"

"Apparently not. She seems to think she can show him."

"Let's just thank our stars it's Steve."

"I agree. It could be a lot worse."

"Do you have to go in tomorrow, Martin?"

"Well yes, I do really. Ted wants to see me."

"Ted! What about? Anything special?"

"Oh no. Just things in general."

"I thought you said he never did anything without a reason."

"Yes, that's true. I expect he has a reason. But I expect I can handle it."

"Of course," he went on, "it's his time of year. Everyone else has gone - to the British Library or to conferences, or just on holiday. The Academic Board ... and the Council ... they won't meet for months. They've passed their last resolutions. It's up to him to implement them ... or not."

"How can he not?"

"Well ... it's a long vacation. Memories are short. He can say it turned out there was no money ... or that there was an unexpected cut ... or that he consulted the Chairman, in view of the circumstances. The trouble is, he enjoys it all!"

"I thought you enjoyed being Dean. Isn't that the same sort of thing?"

"It's not the same. All we do is try to agree on reasonable policies and feed them to him ... for better or worse. And of course, we 'rotate'."

"But isn't that a good idea? Wouldn't it be a good idea for heads of departments to rotate too? Then you could have a rest."

"They can, as a matter of fact, Madge."

"Well, why don't you? Why not take a rest ... for a few years?"

He did not answer.

"Do they really go to the British Library, Martin?"

"I don't think so. It's our joke. Most of my Arts colleagues seem to say that's where they'll be in the vacation. So at closing time you'd expect to be bowled over by the rush. Actually it's just a trickle."

"What about Tony? How's he getting on?"

"He's all right, Madge." She rose and went out of the room. "I must see to dinner: everything's ready."

That day Tony, hearing about Martin's illness, had seemed to be genuinely concerned.

"If I can do anything," he said, "please let me know." He had asked Martin to tell him which responsibilities he should assume, and which he should leave to Martin. Martin could not fault him: he was annoyed at his annoyance.

He went to the dining room. There were only two chairs at the table. The family had chosen their places long before, and had kept them. Now Martin and Madge, occupying their historic positions, faced no-one. As earlier in the bay window, they sat at right angles to each other. It was oddly significant, thought Martin. When the family are together it doesn't show. It'll show more and more now.

"Anyhow, I'm sorry you have to go in, Martin."

Something in her voice caused him to look at her closely, and at last he saw her.

"You're not all right at all, are you, Madge."

She began to weep quietly. He rose and put his arms around her shoulder. It was a familiar gesture, and it caused her to burst into loud weeping.

"Come on, old girl," he said, foolishly.

He waited until she had stopped.

"Now then ..."

She began to serve their portions, dismissing what had happened. He was at a loss, uncertain what to do.

"Why don't we start thinking about a smaller place, Madge?"

"It's not that, Martin."

They went on quietly with their dinner.

"Are you missing the children?"

"Yes of course, I do miss them."

When will I tell him? It'll be some day when we're walking in the park. She knew it would be easier when they were not facing each other - could not face each other. Perhaps at the weekend. They might pass the safe, dull Huttons, arm-in-arm. She began to long for the sympathy which, she was certain, would be a part of what Martin would give her. Even his anger would be worth having.

"Why don't we have a day out, Madge? Not tomorrow, the next day."

"That would be nice, Martin."

"Why not drive down to Sussex. We had nice times there. Walk on the Downs."

She burst into tears again. Puzzled, and uncomfortable, he tried to find a way out for them. He saw that she needed comfort, but did not know how he could give it.

"I'm nearly fifty," she said.

"That's nothing, Madge. I'm *over* fifty."

"It's different for women."

He was glad of the clue, but alarmed by it. Did she seek to revive their marriage? It was the wrong time.

Even if I didn't have Liz, could Madge ever be magic for me? Could she be anything more than the nice, imperfect woman, the sharer of good and bad times, of children, and of years and years? Could that be enough?

"Let's go out somewhere tomorrow. Dinner and a theatre: something like that."

"That would be nice, Martin. Let's." She began to smile a little.

He was relieved that the symptoms, at least, would be attended to. Not for the first time, he would put a cheerful face on it.

He had not seen or spoken to Liz for several weeks, and did not understand her silence. He still hoped there was an explanation: he would not entertain the thought that some other fate, more real than the anguished games of lovers, might have intervened between them.

He remembered a time when they had decided not to see each other again. On a beach, sharing a family holiday, he had ploughed through his misery, trying not to show it, trying to be a father. Now he must try to be a husband.

"Why don't you move back into our room, Martin? I miss your company. You used to say that sleeping together was a strange habit. It's very comforting, though."

"Yes, Madge. I used to think it very odd that two souls would start the night in bodies which happened to be in the same bed, would take off separately, goodness knows where, and then, next morning, would find themselves back in the same bodies, in the same bed."

"I thought you didn't believe in souls."

"Of course I don't, Madge. But you know what I mean."

"What I liked, Martin, was in between. I often woke in the middle of the night. It was always a great comfort if you were there. You might be asleep, and I certainly didn't know where your soul might be. I'm sure I didn't really care. I just liked knowing you were there, if you were in the other bed. If you were in my bed I just liked the warm, bulky thing next to me."

Martin wondered again what were her needs. He was not ready to face the question. He felt sure that she did not guess his. Both were practised in moderating their expression, in finding accommodations, in securing a way of living.

"I sometimes think," went on Madge, "that that must be the worst thing about being widowed. Not being able to have that warm, bulky thing next to you."

"Of course, Madge. I'll move back. I won't be working late for some time. I'm taking it easy." He quoted, with a little irony, the phrase which had been so often quoted to him.

"I realise it's not a great compliment. Calling you a warm, bulky thing, I mean."

"It is a bond, Madge. To have shared a bed over years. Never mind anything else."

"By the way," she said, "I forgot to say - Mr Hutton wants to see you."

"Oh dear! Did he say what about?"

"No. He never does. He seems to think it would be improper to tell me."

Martin sighed.

"But he did look anxious. He was trembling a little, as though he'd had to work himself up."

Martin sighed again. "I'll leave it till the weekend."

Next morning, Friday, when Martin arrived at his office there was a blue envelope on his desk: it was marked 'private'. He saw at once Liz's handwriting. The letter had been misdirected, had come from abroad, and he saw that it had taken a long time to come. At once he felt her presence. In the past, at the beginning of their affair, he had painfully read and re-read her letters, looking for more than was written. He had always done it: but he now knew that letters from girls and women, on their blue paper, in their characteristic, undisciplined styles of handwriting, were not tracts, but gusts of emotion. They had been written quickly, and were not on oath.

He had had fateful letters before; now he wondered what was his fate. The handwriting was nervous and large, the pen inadequate. As always, there were not enough words on the page.

'Darling Martin - I don't know how it happened, but he seems to know about us. We've come to Switzerland. I don't know what he's going to do. We've said so often that we musn't go on that I won't say it again. But that's what I'm afraid of now. Of course, we're having an awful time. Poor Helen! She knows there's something up and pretending she doesn't. She's pretty desperate. So am I. We're spending money like water, and we're all miserable. At least Helen and I are. I never know about him. I wouldn't be surprised if he wasn't enjoying it all. There's been no-one like you, Martin. Your gentleness, strength, intelligence, sharpness, sensitivity, fun - hands - oh dear, I'm making myself cry. I don't know how I'll post this letter. We might be back by the 20th. But God knows when we'll see each other again - yours ever - Liz'

Martin's secretary had come in and stood quietly, discreetly, giving him time to read the letter.

"There's a message from the Provost's secretary," she said. "Could you make it four o'clock instead of two?"

He thought for a moment. "Would you say 'no'. Say that I have to go to Sussex this afternoon."

"Is there anything I ought to get ready for you?"

"No, Jean. I'm not going to the University. I would have told you. I'm going to see an old friend. No need to tell her that, of course."

"I'm sure the Provost won't mind. She was rather apologetic about it and said if you couldn't he'd have to find another day."

She looked anxious. "Professor Blake," she went on, "do you think I could leave early this afternoon? I'll make it up, of course."

"Of course, Jean." She often looked anxious, but he knew nothing about her anxieties. She never allowed them to interfere with her concern for his.

"And could you possibly see Mr Sexton? I told him that you'd be seeing the Provost, but he seemed very anxious to see you."

Martin sighed. "Yes, Jean. I suppose I'd better."

When Sexton came he carried a box. He was trembling with rage- or fear.

"Look at this, Prof!" He opened the box. Inside was the mounted carcase of a bird: it had been damaged.

"Look! *All* of them. Heads screwed off!" He could not go on.

"What a mad thing to do! Who did it? Do you know who did it?"

Sexton continued to tremble.

"Sorry, Prof. I'm afraid you'll have to find that out. It's not my ..." He slowed into silence.

Martin put his hand on Sexton's shoulder. "Does anyone else

know about it?"

Sexton shook his head.

"Only whoever did it."

"Well, Mr Sexton, don't say anything to anyone. I've got to go out this afternoon. I'll see you on Monday and I'll look into it then."

They went into the secretary's room. "Jean, give Mr Sexton a time to see me on Monday."

"Of course." She picked up a diary.

Martin was sure that she had hurriedly put away a handkerchief, that she had been weeping. He wondered whether that, too, would come to him on Monday. Jean, Sexton and the Provost would all have to wait. He put them into that part of his mind.

The arbitrary, pounding traffic frightened Martin. It was not often that traffic worried him, but he was tired, and under par. Years before he had found driving easy: his reflexes, and his London routes, had been quick. But this part of the journey, through the deserts of Brixton, Streatham, Croydon, had become tiresome and boring - nearly intolerable. He turned into a pub car park. He wanted to rest, and to make sure that he had taken his tablets. He was not certain: it seemed to him that his short-term memory was becoming very defective. Just like an absent-minded professor, he thought. Or perhaps it's because they've reduced the pressure. He bought a paper from a pavement stall.

The pub was squalid; he was not sure whether he had been in it before. The conversations around him, dimly overheard, excluded him doubly. He knew that he could not have taken part in them: he would have been bored, and others would have noticed. He had found the same to be true of many common-room conversations. 'Motoring' in that corner, a colleague had said, 'bash the unions' in that. But he had found sympathetic friends, and had valued them: they had given him a platform, a seat.

And yet, he thought, it's comforting only; none of it is magic. It was his sacred word. He thought none of his friends knew about Liz; only his secretary Jean knew, but said nothing, about the occasional blue envelope which arrived on his desk, and about his occasional, undefined journeys and absences.

"You all right, man?" said a man sitting at his table: he was black.

"Yes, thank you. I'm all right. Why ...?"

"Only you're spilling your beer."

"So I am. I didn't notice. I was reading the paper." He had already exhausted it.

"Can I look at it a minute? Just the back pages."

"Of course. Carry on."

Martin took Liz's letter from his pocket and read it again, amazed at its power to create her. He had kept all her letters: they were in his desk at home - packed, with other *memorabilia* of their affair, in a single, large envelope. I really ought to get rid of it, he thought, or put it in the bank, or something like that. He would not want it to be found after his death, even though that outcome, by its nature, was infinitely distant.

Suspended, uncertain of the future, he reminded himself of some of the unhappinesses of his life. The worst - against which all others must be measured - had been on the death of his father. He had been ineffective as a father, and no match for his wife; he had not, in his last years, seemed to be significant in the lives of his children. He was someone to be visited, to be compensated for past unkindnesses, to be listened to. None of them could have guessed at the strength of his hold upon them, at the pain they would suffer at its removal. None would have thought of him as a support: all felt weakened by its loss. None quite knew what he had felt for him: all found that it had been love.

Martin saw that it explained his other unhappinesses: their occasions had been the illnesses of his children or the endings - or presumed endings - of love affairs. Because the children recovered these were finally not remembered. The others could never quite disappear.

Sometimes the girl - or woman - had gone to another. Perhaps she would come back but go again: the second pain was as bad as the first. His affair with Madge had been thus turbulent. With Liz the endings had been agreed by both: it was no easier to bear. Nothing made any difference to that pain.

He remembered one girl: she had been twenty, he was older. If he had captured her he would have secured her by marriage: it had still been the prize which could be offered. But she, though herself tortured by it, had gone to another. His friends had tried to comfort him with flippancy. He still remembered, over the decades, his overwhelming, shattering, continuing dismay - at the thought that they would never meet again. The young, adorable, irreplaceable girl was as though dead. Would it have been easier if she had died? He was not sure.

The shape which the ending revealed was the negative of that which had been joyfully built: the pain of the ending was the negative of the strange excitement of the beginning. The end showed what had been.

That affair had started quickly: both had seemed to be excited, optimistic and expectant. But within weeks she had, by chance, met the other, and *he* had excited her. She had told Martin, and, for a time, they continued to meet. He struggled to hold her, offering a reduced commitment. Only later, when she had gone, and he could measure his feeling for her, had he understood how she must feel for the other, and why she had been right to dismiss him. It would have been easier if he could have thought her motives trivial, or superficial, but he knew that they were not.

One day she had failed to arrive at the arranged meeting place. For hours he waited, or watched the place. But she did not come. He waited for her to act. At last her letter came: it was kind, generous, but its message was final. She would not see him again. For months he had rehearsed the emotions of the jilted lover. Surely, he thought, she cannot know how I'm suffering.

He remembered another. This one had left him but had remained within sight: all three worked in the same laboratory. So, watching the trim body which he had held, listening to the gentle voice which had spoken love words to him, he had been forced to hide what he felt, and it was the more intense because she was within sight. The ordinariness of what he saw and heard - she might be standing among colleagues, drinking tea, or discussing a laboratory routine - made it no easier. He did not see her as the young scientist, only as the lover who had left him. He had not felt jealousy, only loss.

They had been significant experiences. Perhaps everyone had suffered in the same way. He knew that among groups of people around tea-urns there could be tragedy.

Once or twice he had been the one to perform the execution: the girls had seemed to accept their fate honourably. Had they suffered as much? Later he knew that they had: the loser must. He had indeed been told that women suffered more. In his questing days he had not thought that possible.

Was he now to repeat the experience? Would it still be as bad? He was sure that he had not changed, that he was as capable of suffering as he had been at twenty.

He put Liz's letter in his pocket, and left the pub.

*

Sometimes, he thought, ideas come so quickly that I couldn't write them down, even if I wanted to.

It's a sort of tense placidity we've had all these years.

In pursuing a woman victory is within sight as soon as she allows you to win the smallest battle - as soon as she admits she is open to pursuit, or is being pursued. She might say 'stay and have another cup', or 'how would I ever get to talk to anyone interesting?'

What does he think we ought to do? Sit at opposite ends of the table, both being Chairman!

She'd sometimes say: 'why didn't you tell me?' I'd say: 'I've told you a hundred times. I'm always telling you'. We never got past that.

Every woman's face has a sentence written on it.
    It won't be you
    I am not here
    Come
    Come if you dare: it will be worth it
    Do not trouble: it is not worth it
    Sometimes all it says is: I really must be going.

There's nothing more meaningless - even obscene - than a row of chorus girls, kicking and dancing. The better they do it the more obscene it is. It destroys bodies and even faces. Of course, when they sing, it's ridiculously moving. I suppose it's because they can't.

When she put her hand on my arm, I'd been telling her about Edward, when he'd been ill. Odd that I've suddenly remembered.

People introduced to you sometimes start talking as though you were in the middle of a conversation already.

One's subconscious is always busy, weighing up where you and the woman stand in the pecking order. If she's too far above you don't notice her. If just above, have a go. If below, don't bother.

It's odd that he can't bring himself to call me 'Martin' - unless there's someone else there. When we're alone together he calls me nothing at all, just 'I say.'

I used to hate her saying: 'I can't leave him: you're stronger than he is.'

We used to have almost ceremonial final partings. We'd go to a theatre, or something, and agree that neither would indicate, during the whole evening, that it was the last time.

If you put a DO NOT DISTURB notice on a hotel door, could you stay for ever?

I suppose a couple could be incompatible in kitchen habits.

I've never been able to understand the amazing courtesy of people who let you give them orders, or teach them.

When a glassblower makes something he sometimes turns it upside down and you see that what you'd thought was the real thing is to be cut off and thrown away - and had been only a handle. 'Nothing to it,' he says.

How is my life really divided between the open and the secret? Is it 80:20, or 20:80? Some people would say 'overt' and 'covert'. They're not my sort of words. Neither is 'albeit'.

When she says 'I'm exactly what I seem to be,' she wants you to find out why it's not true.

When we used to go to the Carol Service, with the Home Secretary taking the collection, and the Vicar blessing everybody, I sometimes wished that everything really was like that.

*

How rarely the spirit of delight actually comes! And how elusive. Sometimes I'm not even sure it's been near.

Surely everyone here must be thinking the same thoughts. Why do we each have to think it out separately? Why is it not written down somewhere? I've often wondered about that.

What is that man doing? Isn't he the one who borrowed my paper?

What is that ambulance doing there?

I would like to be on that mountain again.

I would like to talk to my father again - not to know what he has to say, but to pretend that I want to know.

I would like to be with those two plump vegetable sellers again, and their mother.

I would like to know what Edward thinks all the time.

I would like all those traumas of adult life to be wiped out. I would take them out, one by one, and find they no longer had any power.

I would like to walk up and down Sleazy Street, and find my very own magazine in a shop.

I would like to hear a long, pure, steady note - on a flute, or an oboe.

I would like to go on a quest, not to find whatever is at the end of it, but to find out what I want to find.

I would like all those girls, middle-aged now, to be young again.

The lovely, moist grass pressed against his cheek.

He was curiously happy.

I would like to walk up and down Sleazy Street, and find my very own magazine in a shop.

I would like to hear a long, pure, steady note - on a flute, or an oboe.

I would like to go on a quest, not to find whatever is at the end of it, but to find out what I want to find.

I would like all those girls, middle-aged now, to be young again.

The lovely, moist grass pressed against his cheek.

He was curiously happy.